More titles in the Alice series

Agony of Alice
Alice in Rapture, Sort of!
Reluctantly Alice
All But Alice
Alice, Woman of the Home
Alice in Between
Alice the Brave
Alice in Lace
Outrageously Alice
The Grooming of Alice
Alice on the Outside

Look out for

Simply Alice

All Simon and Schuster Books are available by post from:
Simon & Schuster Cash Sales. PO Box 29
Douglas, Isle of Man IM99 1BQ
Credit cards accepted.
Please telephone 01624 836000
fax 01624 670923, Internet
http://www.bookpost.co.uk or email:
bookshop@enterprise.net for details

aLice

Alice Alone

Patrick
+
Pony
X

by Phyllis Reynolds Naylor

POCKET BOOKS

To the memory of my former editor,
Jean Karl, who helped me raise Alice,
and who taught me as much about life
as she taught me about writing

CAVAN COUNTY LIBRARY
ACC. No. C/.1.9.7.3.9.5.
CLASS No. ....5/.12.-.14.
INVOICE NO. ....7012.2.
PRICE......€.6.:.61.

POCKET BOOKS

First published in the UK in 2004 by Pocket Books
An imprint of Simon and Schuster UK Ltd
Africa House, 64-78 Kingsway, London WC2B 6AH
A Viacom Company

First published in the USA by Simon & Schuster Children's Publishing
Copyright © 2001 by Phyllis Reynolds Naylor
Cover design by Blacksheep © 2004 Simon & Schuster

All rights reserved, including the right to reproduce this book or portions
thereof in any form whatsoever.

A CIP catalogue record for this book is available from the British Library
POCKET BOOKS and colophon are registered trademarks of Simon & Schuster

ISBN 0 743 46903 8

1 3 5 7 9 10 8 6 4 2

Printed by Bookmarque, Croydon, Surrey.

Contents

CAVAN COUNTY
LIBRARY

1

Homecoming

September has always felt more like New Year to me than January first. It's such a brand-new start – new classes, new friends, new teachers, new clothes . . . This September I was entering a school almost twice the size of our old one, and it was scary to think about being one of the youngest kids again. I hated the thought that I wouldn't be considered sophisticated anymore, and I'd probably feel as awkward as I used to.

"Hey, no sweat!" Lester, my soon-to-be-twenty-two-year-old brother said. "You'll get used to it in no time – the left-over hospital food, the –"

"What?" I said. We were sitting out on the front steps sharing a bag of microwave popcorn on the very last day of August. In fact, we'd just made a lunch of hot dogs and popcorn.

"Didn't you know?" he said. "The food in the school is left-over stuff from the prison canteen. But it won't kill you. Of course, there isn't any hot water in the showers, and –"

"What?" I bleated again.

"And the showers, you know, are mixed."

"Lester!" I scolded. If anything would drive my friend Elizabeth to an all-girls' school, it was rumours like that.

"Hey, look around you," Lester said, taking another handful of popcorn and spilling some on the steps. "Do you realise that practically every person you meet over the age of eighteen went through years ten to thirteen and lived to tell about it?"

"I know I'll survive, Les, but when I think of all the embarrassing things I'll probably do, all the humiliating stuff just waiting to happen . . ."

"But what about all the good stuff? The *great* stuff? What's the next good thing on your agenda, for example?"

"Dad coming home this afternoon."

"See? What else?"

"Patrick gets back on Saturday."

"There you are," Lester said.

He was being pretty nice to me, I decided, considering that he'd just broken up with his latest girlfriend, Eva, for which I was secretly glad, because I don't think she was his type. She certainly wasn't mine. She had starved herself skinny and was always finding fault with Lester. If they ever married, I figured it would be only a matter of, time before she started criticising me.

"Are you picking Dad up?" I asked. Lester's working on a master's degree in philosophy at the University of Maryland. His summer school courses were finished, but he works part-time.

"Yeah. I got the afternoon off from the shoe store.

I figured Dad deserves a welcoming committee. Want to come?"

"Yes. But first I want to bake him something," I said.

I'd already bought the ingredients because I'd planned this cake in advance. I once found a note on a recipe card of Mum's for pineapple upside-down cake, saying it was Dad's favourite, so I decided to make that.

Mum died of leukaemia when I was in nursery school, so it's just been Dad and Lester and me ever since. Except that Dad's going to marry my former English teacher, Sylvia Summers, who's in England for a year on an exchange programme, and Dad was just coming back from a two-week trip to see her. *One* of the reasons Miss Summers went to England was to give her time to decide between Dad and Jim Sorringer, the deputy head back in my old school. She and Jim dated for a long time – until she met Dad. But I guess she decided she didn't need a year to think it over after all, because when Dad went to visit her, they became engaged.

Pineapple upside-down cake is really easy, especially if you use a cake mix. All you do is melt some butter in a large baking tin, stir in a cup of brown sugar, add canned pineapple slices, and then the cake mix. I had the phone tucked under my ear and was explaining all this to Pamela, my other "best" friend, while I worked.

"... and when you take it out of the oven, you,

turn the tin upside down on a big plate." And then I added, "Why don't you make one for *your* dad? Surprise him." If ever a girl and her dad needed to learn to get along, it was Pamela and Mr Jones. Ever since Pamela's mum ran off with her personal trainer Pamela's been angry with both her parents, but she and her dad are trying hard to make it work.

"Maybe I will," said Pamela. "You have any pineapple I could borrow?"

"I think so," I said.

"We may not have enough butter."

"You could borrow that, too."

"Brown sugar?"

"Well . . . maybe."

"Would you happen to have a cake mix?"

"Pamela!" I said.

"Never mind. I'll go to the shop," she told me.

While the cake was baking, I did a quick clean-up of the house. I dusted the tops of all the furniture, ran a carpet sweeper over the rug, made the beds, and wiped out the sinks – sort of like counting to one hundred by fives, skipping all the numbers in between.

Lester did the laundry and the dishes, just so the place wouldn't smell like sour milk and dirty socks when Dad walked in. Miss Summers always has the most wonderful scent, and I could guarantee that her flat in England didn't stink.

Of course, what I wanted most to know was where Dad had been sleeping while he was there, but I'm old enough now that I don't just pop those questions at him. I'll admit I've imagined the two of them having sex, though. If I ever get near the topic, he says, "Al!" My full name is Alice Kathleen McKinley, but Dad and Lester call me Al.

We had things pretty much in order by 3:45 – the cake cooling on the counter, the laundry folded and put away. I decided to put on something a little more feminine than my old cut-off jeans, so I dressed in a purple tank top and a sheer cotton skirt. It was lavender with little purple and yellow flowers all over it, yards and yards of gauzy material that swished and swirled about my legs when I walked. I stood in front of the mirror, whirling around, and the skirt billowed out in a huge circle. Even Lester was impressed when he saw me.

"Madame?" he said, holding out his arm, and we descended grandly down the front steps.

Dad's plane was landing at Dulles International Airport, so we had to drive way over into Virginia to pick him up. I sat beside Lester, my legs crossed at the knees, feeling very alluring and grown-up. I was wearing string sandals, and my toenails were painted dusky rose.

"It's going to be awkward, isn't it, after Miss Summers moves in," I said as Lester expertly navigated the carriageway.

"I can't eat breakfast in my boxer shorts anymore, I'll tell you that," he said.

"I guess she won't exactly be eating breakfast in *her* underwear, either," I said. "Gosh, Lester, I hardly even remember Mum. I don't know what it's like to have a woman around, I'm so used to being the only female in the house."

"Don't feel sorry for you, feel sorry for *me*," said Lester. "Imagine having *two* females here, taking over!"

The plane was going to be fifty minutes late, we discovered when we got to the airport, so Lester bought us two giant-size lemonades. We sat on a high stool in a little bar while we drank them, my feet crossed at the ankles, and my four-tiered skirt cascading all the way down to the floor.

Then we ambled around, looking in shops, until I realised that the lemonade was going right through me.

Lester waited outside the toilets, and when I came out again, I told him I wanted to check out a little gift shop I'd seen earlier. I was already thinking of what to buy Miss Summers for Christmas, and hurried on ahead so I could look around before Dad's plane came in. Two guys, maybe a year older than I, came up behind me and, as they passed, one of them said, "Cute butterflies."

What? I thought.

An older man passed on the other side of me and smiled.

Then, "Al," came Lester's voice. "Wait."

I glanced around and saw Lester walking rapidly up behind me.

"Stop!" he whispered urgently, taking hold of my arm, and I felt the fingers of his other hand fumbling with the waistband of my underwear.

"Lester!" I said, jerking away from him, but he gave a final tug, and suddenly I realised I had walked out of the toilet with the hem of my skirt caught in the waistband of my yellow butterfly bikinis.

"Oh, my God!" I cried, covering my face with both hands as several more people walked by us smiling.

"Just pretend it happens every day," Lester commanded, urging me forward again.

"Everyone *saw!*" I croaked, feeling the heat of my face against my palms.

"Al," he said, "people are far more interested in catching a plane than they are in your underpants. The world does *not* revolve around you. Keep walking."

I uncovered my eyes. "Is this what it's going to be like living with a philosopher?"

He shrugged. "Would you rather go the rest of your life with your hands over your face?"

I took a deep breath, and we made our way to the gate.

We had to wait till Dad went through customs, of course, and then he would take a shuttle to the main terminal. But at last the passengers were coming up the ramp and through the exit, and there he was in his rumpled shirt, a wrinkled jacket thrown over his arm, a trace of beard on his face, a man without sleep. But I don't think I'd ever seen him look so happy.

I threw my arms around him as Les reached out for his carry-on bag.

"Oh, Dad!" I said.

"Home!" he sighed in my ear. "And what a welcome! Good of you to meet me, Les!" Then he and Lester hugged.

"Bet you're ready for some sleep," Les said, grinning.

"The bed will feel pretty good, all right," said Dad. "How *are* you guys, anyway?"

We chattered all the way down the escalator to the baggage claim area, and Dad and I watched for his nylon bag to come around the conveyor belt while Les went to get the car.

"So what do you think, Al?" Dad asked, grinning at me as we retrieved his bag, then leaned against the wall by an exit, waiting for Lester. "Think you'll get along with your new mum?"

"Oh, Dad, it's the most wonderful news in the world," I said. "You don't know how long I've wanted you and Miss Summers to get engaged. I can't wait!"

"Neither can we. This separation's going to be hard, but we'll manage," he said.

"Will you be getting married next June?"

"July, maybe. We haven't worked out all the details yet." He gave my shoulder a squeeze. "So how did you and Lester get along without me?"

"Okay. He broke up with Eva, you know. And Marilyn's back in the picture. Sort of. They're just friends, Lester says."

"Well, that's good. I've always liked Marilyn. Is Patrick back yet?"

"Saturday," I told him.

I asked him about Miss Summers's flat in England,

and he described the rooms, and what the town of Chester looked like, and then we saw Lester's car pull up outside.

I crawled in the back and let Dad have the passenger seat. But there was so much to tell. As Lester drove, I rattled on about how Aunt Sally had flown over from Chicago to make sure Lester and I were okay, and how we got her to leave again, and how Pamela had gone to Colorado to live with her mother, then come back again to be with her dad, and how I got my string sandals at a half-price sale, and . . .

"Al," said Les.

I stopped. "What?" Was I acting like the world revolved around me again?

He nodded towards Dad. Dad's head was leaning against the window, and he was sound asleep. Smiling, still.

Elizabeth and Pamela and I sat on my sofa Saturday afternoon, our bare feet propped on the coffee table, gluing little transfers to our toenails. Elizabeth was putting roses on hers, I was gluing stars, and Pamela was gluing on signs of the zodiac.

"I don't know," I said. "We may just look freakish. Maybe you don't wear toenail decorations after year nine."

"Are you kidding?" said Pamela. "We can do anything we want. You'll see all kinds of stuff. You can be as old-fashioned or individual as you like."

"I thought we *were* individual," I said. Pamela now had a blue streak right down the middle of her short blonde hair. It made her head look sort of like a horse's mane. Elizabeth would probably have to be tortured before she would do anything to her long dark hair.

"So if we're individuals, why are the three of us sitting here all gluing transfers on our toenails?" Elizabeth asked.

"Good question," I said.

She leaned back and stared at her feet. "I'm scared," she told us. "I'm afraid I'll get lost and be late to class or I'll wander into some part of the school reserved for seniors or I'll start my period and the toilets will be out of towels, or –"

"Elizabeth, shut up," said Pamela. "If you're going to begin year ten no different than you were when you started year eight, then what's the point?"

I gave Pamela a look, because Elizabeth went through a sort of anorexic period over the summer, and we think she's beginning to pull out of it, but we're not sure. I didn't want Pamela to say anything that would set her off again.

"What she means is you've got too many big things going for you to worry about all the small stuff," I told Elizabeth. "Lester says if you just look around, you'll realise that almost everybody over the age of eighteen . . ." I stopped right then, because my eye caught something moving outside the window, and when I looked out, I saw Patrick riding up on the lawn on his bike.

"It's Patrick!" I cried, thinking he wasn't due back till evening. I grabbed my can of Sprite and sloshed some around in my mouth before I got up and went out on the porch to meet him.

He looked as though he'd grown another inch – taller, somehow, in his white Polo shirt and khaki shorts. Patrick has red hair, so he doesn't really tan, but his skin looked a deeper red. "Hi," he said, smiling at me.

"Hi," I said, feeling shy all of a sudden.

"You wanted me to bring you the perfect shell," he said, handing me a little box.

"Is it? Really?" I lifted the lid.

It was a beautiful shell, curved at one end, a beige colour with little white spots all over it, and ivory on the inside.

"It's not perfect," he said, pointing out a small chip on the edge, "but it was the best I could find." Then he pulled me towards him. "How about the perfect kiss?"

I loved the feel of his arms around me. It was broad daylight there on the porch, but I didn't care. I put my arms around his neck and turned my face up to his. He pressed his lips against mine – softly at first, then hard and firm, and his fingers spread out across my back. It was a long, slow, beautiful, kiss.

He let me go long enough to breathe, and asked, "Well, how was it?"

"It'll do," I said, and we kissed again.

"Ahhhhhhhhh!" came a long, loud sigh from the window. We jerked around in time to see two heads disappearing, one brunette, one blonde, followed by the rapid thud of footsteps going upstairs.

2

Getting Started

For my first day in year ten, I wore a necklace that Dad and Miss Summers had picked out together. It was a black velvet ribbon that hooked at the back, worn snugly around the neck, covered with antique lace and tiny dewdrop pearls sewn here and there. It was just right to go with the scoop-neck black jersey top I'd chosen to wear on my first day with a great pair of jeans. I thought I looked stunning.

"Don't I look ravishing, Lester?" I asked, standing in his doorway.

Lester lifted one eyebrow as he sorted through his shirts. "How come the top half of you looks like it's going to a party and the bottom half looks like you're going fishing?" he asked.

"It's the style, Lester!" I said. "I'd look like a geek if everything matched."

"Is that why one ear's lower than the other?' he said.

"What?" I asked, walking over to the mirror.

"And one eye's crooked?"

"*Lester!*"

"Hey, relax. It's only school, not the army. Dad

never told you he got you on sale, huh? Fifty percent off."

I gave him a look and went down to breakfast. Dad was eating a bowl of Weetabix.

"You look great, Al," he told me. "Black's a good colour on you. Sylvia said it would be."

"Were you and Sylvia shopping together?" I asked. "For a ring, perhaps?"

"As a matter of fact, we were," he said, and smiled over his cereal.

"Describe it,' I said eagerly.

"Well, it's round, of course."

"The *diamond*," I said. "Is it one large stone, or . . .?"

"It isn't a diamond at all, Al. We chose matching gold bands, sort of a woven look."

I stopped chewing. "You didn't buy Sylvia a diamond?"

"No. She said she didn't want to feel responsible for it. She said she'd be continually checking to see if it was still there, and it would catch on things –"

"But . . . but diamonds are forever!" I squeaked. "Enduring love!"

"What's this, a singing commercial?" Lester asked, coming into the kitchen.

"She's upset because I didn't buy Sylvia a diamond," Dad told him. "When you get married, Al, you can have diamonds on your toes, for all I care. You can even have a diamond in your navel. But Sylvia and I wanted matching gold bands."

"So she doesn't have any kind of an engagement ring?" I asked.

"No. Just a wedding band, after we're married."

I took another bite of cereal and thought it over. "Well, at least you'll *both* be wearing them. I'm suspicious of any man who wants his wife to wear a ring but won't wear one himself. Now maybe Janice Sherman will understand that you are really, truly taken." Janice Sherman is assistant manager at the Melody Inn, where Dad's manager, and she's had a crush on him ever since we moved to Silver Spring.

Dad merely grunted, and turned to the editorial page. "Watch the clock, Al," he said. "You have to catch the bus ten minutes earlier, remember."

I'd already been shown around the school. All the new kids in year ten had gone to school for a half day to find our classrooms and try our lockers and get a floor plan of the whole school. But we weren't nervous about locks and floor plans; we were nervous about the kids in year eleven, year twelve and year thirteen, and today they'd be out in force.

Elizabeth was already waiting when I got outside. The new bus stop was several streets away, so we'd be walking together. She was wearing her long dark hair pulled back away from her face, with a few curls hanging down at the temples, and the rest scooped up with a scrunchie at the back. Elizabeth's got the most gorgeous skin and eyelashes and, except for shoulders and knees that still look too bony, she's beautiful, only she'd never believe it.

"You look great," I told her, eyeing her royal blue shirt and off-white jeans.

But she was looking at my collar necklace "Where'd you get it?"

"Dad and Sylvia gave it to me. She chose it, I'll bet. They were shopping for wedding bands."

"Then it's official," Elizabeth said. "Gosh, Alice, aren't you excited?"

"It's still a long way off," I told her. "Right now I'm excited about year ten!"

"Well, I'm nervous!" Elizabeth said.

Except for algebra and possibly Spanish, I didn't think there would be any subject I couldn't handle this year, but Elizabeth is pretty wired about marks. She's always had good ones, of course – better than either Pamela's or mine. But from year ten on, we'd heard, your marks appear on your report when you apply to college, and Elizabeth kept saying she had "too much on her plate," which was an interesting way of putting it.

"I've made up my mind," she said as we crossed the first street. "I'm giving up ballet and taking modern dance instead. It's much less rigid, and it will be enough to keep me exercising without having to audition for *The Nutcracker* every year." She'd already given up gymnastics last spring, and tap the year before.

"If it's what you really want to do," I told her.

"But I also want to drop piano, and that upsets my folks. I just don't like that practise hanging over me every day. Mum wants me to start with a new teacher. She says I've outgrown Mrs Ralston, and I'm probably just bored, so she's signed me up with Mr

Hedges, who's supposed to be the best in Silver Spring."

"Well it's up to you," I said again.

"I told Mum I'd take a couple of lessons just to see, but I already know how I feel about it. They just act so . . . so *disappointed* in me . . ."

It's not easy being Elizabeth, I know. She'd been an only child for thirteen years of her life – until Nathan Paul was born last year – so she'd had her parents' whole attention – adoration, really – all to herself. At the same time, they expect a lot of her, or maybe she just demands a lot of herself in order to please them – but she's had about every kind of lesson there is and wants to be good at everything. And perhaps she's just beginning to realise how impossible that is.

At the bus stop there were some older kids we didn't know, but when the bus came, a lot of our crowd was already on, and they were laughing.

"There's Alice," I heard someone say. I wondered what the big deal was and looked around for Patrick, and then I saw him in the third row, with a short, curly-haired girl sitting in his lap. Patrick was laughing, too, and his face was red.

I stared. It was Penny, the new girl who had worked at the ice-cream shop over the summer, the place we went to hang out, the dimpled girl the guys liked to tease.

"Oh, Patrick, you're in for it now!" Brian hollered.

Penny looked around, then bounced off Patrick's lap, her eyes dancing. "Oops!" she said apologetically to me. "Sorry, but I was pushed."

"Mark pushed her," called out Jill.

I didn't know what to say, so I just laughed, too, and sat down beside Patrick.

"She sort of fell on me," he explained.

The kids from the years above were watching us with bored amusement, like we were a playpen full of toddlers. I gave Patrick a quick kiss. "Were you able to change your lunch to fourth lesson?" I asked.

"No. I couldn't swing it."

"Oh, Patrick! We won't be eating together!" I said.

"I know, but with the accelerated programme I'll have to grab a sandwich when I can."

Patrick had mentioned the possibility of an accelerated programme before, but in such an offhand way, it hadn't really sunk in. "You're actually going to do it? The last four years of school in three?"

"If I can hack it."

"*Why?*"

"So I can get a jump on things. Go to college one year earlier, get out one year earlier, get a job, make a start –"

"What's the hurry?" I asked.

"Life," said Patrick.

"But *this* is life, too! What about all the fun stuff in school? What about the leavers' dance? You won't even be here!" What I was really asking was, *What about me?*

"So I'll come back for the dance," Patrick said, smiling. "Wherever I am, I'll come back and take you to the dance. Okay?"

That was a commitment if ever I heard one. I

slipped my fingers through his, and he caressed my thumb the way I like, and I was very happy to see that Penny noticed and looked the other way.

I'm not very good at maths and science. Dad's not either, actually. Lester's probably better at both than we are, but one of the reasons I'd been dreading year ten was algebra. I'd put off taking it as long as I could, but anyone expecting to go to college had to pass it: algebra, geometry, physics. I got stomachaches just thinking about it. Patrick said he'd help, though. Patrick, the whiz-at-everything guy.

Biology I could handle, though. It made pictures in my mind that algebra didn't. U.S. history I could handle. English. Even Spanish, I discovered. Then there was PE. and PHSE, and, for my extra-curricular stuff, I signed up to be one of the year ten roving reporters for the school newspaper, *The Edge*. I'd even be able to take photos sometimes. Pamela signed up for the drama club, and so did I. Except she wanted a leading role, and I wanted to be part of the stage crew.

I sailed through most of the day, all right. The only class I had with Pamela was history, and the only ones I had with Elizabeth were PHSE and PE. None with Patrick. It was the lunch hour that I missed him most, though. A lot of our old gang was there, so we grabbed a table for ourselves, but I felt odd man out without Patrick.

"Hey, listen!" Karen called from her end of the table. "How about a mixed pyjama party, my place, Saturday night.

"Mixed?" I asked

"Yes. *Every*body! Bring a sleeping bag and we'll take over the living room."

"Cool!" said Brian. "Your mum going to be there?"

"Of course!"

"Dam!" said Brian, and we laughed.

"She won't mind," said Karen. Her folks are divorced, and she spends every other weekend at her father's. I figured her mum was just trying to make the weekends Karen spent with her extra special.

But Elizabeth was still staring at Karen. "Everyone on the floor together?" she asked.

"Well, I suppose the girls could lie on top of the guys, if you'd prefer," Pamela joked. Everybody laughed. Sometimes I wish Pamela wouldn't do that – embarrass Elizabeth in front of everyone.

"We had a mixed pyjama party at our church once," Karen explained. "Our youth group had this project – we were going to scrub down all the pews in the sanctuary and repolish them – so we had an overnight first, and then the minister and his wife made breakfast for us the next morning and we cleaned the pews."

"Hey, the library had one when I was in year seven," Brian told us. "They called it a Read-all-Night-athon, and about fifty kids showed up. There were sleeping bags over the whole floor. They turned out the lights at one in the morning, though."

I liked the idea of sleeping on the floor next to Patrick. Sleeping *anywhere* next to Patrick, actually. I told him about it after school.

"Ummm," he said, putting his arm around me and kissing my hair.

Everyone seemed to be in a good mood at dinner that evening. Dad had been on cloud nine since he got back from England, and Lester came home from the university to say that he got a real "babe" for a professor in his Schopenhauer course. I was in a good mood because Dad had bought a Chinese take away for dinner, and the whole kitchen smelled of prawns in garlic sauce.

"Have you told Janice Sherman about your engagement yet?" I asked Dad.

He chewed thoughtfully for a moment. "Guess I haven't. I did mention it to Marilyn because she more or less asked. What she asked was if Sylvia and I were still an 'item,' which is a strange way of putting it, I think, so naturally I told her we were engaged."

I studied my father. There are times he seems to be living on a different planet entirely. "Dad, Janice Sherman has been your assistant manager for . . . what? Seven years? Marilyn has been a part-time employee for maybe one, and you told Marilyn before you told Janice. *Why?*"

"Self-preservation," Lester murmured, looking amused.

Dad seemed perplexed. "Because Janice didn't *ask*," he said. "She asked what it was like in Chester, so I described the countryside. I thought that's what she wanted to know."

I flung back my head and screeched at the ceiling. "Dad, you are so *dense!* Janice Sherman doesn't care about Chester, she cares about you! She doesn't want to know what you and Sylvia did in the countryside, she really wants to know what you did under the covers."

"Al!" Dad said. "Now that's just –!"

"It's true! She only asked about the countryside because she thought maybe she could learn how serious the relationship is."

"Well, now, how am I supposed to know *that?*" Dad shot back. "If a woman asks me if there are as many sheep in England as the postcards make them out to be, how am I supposed to know she's really asking about Sylvia?"

Lester laughed. "Because the woman's had a major crush on you since day one," he said.

"Major, *major!*" I added. "Dad, if you ever asked Janice Sherman to marry you, she'd be in a bridal gown by six that evening."

"You two are exaggerating," Dad said. "Janice may have had a mild interest in me at one time, but she's dated a number of men over the years."

"Mostly music instructors there at the Melody Inn just to make you jealous," I told him.

"Nonsense," said Dad. "Anyway, Marilyn seemed quite happy about it." He smiled. "What she said was, 'It'll be nice to have someone sharing your pillow again, Mr M., won't it?' Now in my day I wouldn't have dared say something like that to my boss."

"That's Marilyn!" said Lester, and all three of us laughed.

And then I did the stupidest thing. With all this talk of sharing pillows, I brought up the mixed pyjama party. "Well, guess what I'm going to do on Saturday? I'm going to a mixed pyjama party," I said, my brain on holiday.

And without missing a beat, Dad said, "Over my dead body."

"Everyone's going to be there – the whole gang."

"Everyone but you. I don't care if the Pope and all his cardinals will be there. You are not going to a mixed pyjama party. I never heard of such a dumb idea," Dad said.

"Al, *I* never went to a mixed pyjama party," Lester said, siding with Dad.

I couldn't believe that things could go downhill so fast. One minute we'd all been eating fried rice and talking about Dad's engagement, and the next minute the bottom had dropped out of my world.

I had promised myself that when I started year ten I was going to act more mature. When Dad and I disagreed about something, I was going to discuss it with him calmly. No more breaking into tears and running upstairs to slam my door. So what did I do? Break into tears. All I could think of was that everyone would be there – *Patrick* would be there, probably – and I wouldn't.

"I can't believe you!" I sobbed. "Y-you don't know anything about it, *either* of you. You just have these knee-jerk reactions, and think that just because a bunch of kids are in sleeping bags, something's going to happen."

My outburst took us all by surprise, I guess. We'd all been feeling mellow, and now this. But if *I* wasn't sleeping on the floor next to Patrick, who would be?

"Al," Dad said, trying to sound reasonable. "What adults in their right minds would allow a bunch of fourteen-year-old boys and girls to spend the night together? *Think!*"

"Churches do it! Libraries do it! It's no big deal," I told him, wiping my eyes and trying to sound more grown up. "All you can think about is sex! Everyone simply brings a sleeping bag and we watch TV and eat popcorn and talk and play cards, and then everyone goes to sleep in their own sleeping bag. Do you actually think some guy is going to crawl into a girl's bag with a dozen other kids lying only two feet away?"

"At two o'clock in the morning in a dark room? Yep!" put in Lester.

I turned on him then. "Karen said her church group had one and they all got up the next morning and scrubbed down the pews."

"What'd they do the night before? Have a food fight?" Lester asked.

"No! It was a work project, but they started with a pyjama party. Mark said the public library had one when he was in year seven, and the librarians slept right there with the kids."

Dad sighed. "So what adult is going to sleep on the floor with you?"

"Karen's mum, I suppose."

"Where's her father?"

"They're divorced."

"Al, if you are going to be sleeping on the floor with a bunch of guys around, it's going to be under *our* roof, not off in some divorced mother's apartment where things could get beyond her control."

I hardly even stopped for breath. "Then can we have the party here?"

Dad blinked.

"We've got more room than Karen, we wouldn't be sleeping so close together, and if you want you can sit on the sofa all night with a broom and poke anyone who gets out of line," I said, knowing full well that Dad can't stay awake very long.

Lester looked at Dad. "She's gotcha there, Pop."

Dad looked as though he'd just been hit with a brick. "Al, I am going to count the days until you leave for college," he said, half under his breath.

"How do you know I won't live at home and go to the University of Maryland like Lester?" I chirped.

He turned helplessly to Lester.

Les shrugged. "I don't know. If churches and libraries do it . . ."

"Even *Elizabeth* can do it!" I said, not at all sure.

At that precise moment, like a message from God, the phone rang, and when I picked it up in the hall, Karen said, "Alice, Mum won't let me have the party. I can't believe this! I was sure she'd say yes."

"I'll call you back," I said quickly, and hung up.

"Okay, Lester, you've got to help me out here," Dad

was saying. "Al can have the party, and I'll make the popcorn and order the pizza, but after I go to bed, you're in charge."

"What?" yelled Lester.

"You know I can't stay awake past eleven. It's a Saturday night, your classes have only just begun at Uni, so you can't have too much to do yet. I need you. Once Sylvia and I get married, we'll handle things like this."

Lester gave a howl of pain.

"Thanks, Dad," I said.

I went upstairs and phoned Karen. "The party's still on. Dad says we can have it here."

"Really?" she cried. "Oh, Alice, your dad is so cool!"

3

A Sudden Announcement

Once the word got out that Lester was in charge, everyone, it seemed, was coming. Even Elizabeth. We got a lot of calls, though – parents wanting to talk to Dad to make sure he was going to be here. This only made Dad more nervous, and Lester berserk.

"I really appreciate this, Les," I said. "Maybe I can make it up to you somehow."

"You can hire ten vestal virgins to massage my feet and feed me grapes, but you'll still owe me," he growled.

As Elizabeth and I walked to the bus stop the next morning, she said, "Mum said I could come if I put my sleeping bag next to Lester and not off in some dark corner with one of the guys."

"Poor Les," I said. "And to think his birthday's on Sunday."

Elizabeth stopped walking. "His birthday's Sunday?"

"So?" I said.

"Alice, we've got to get him a cake! He's giving up one whole night of his life just for us."

Every day is sacred to Elizabeth Price. She knows

exactly what she plans to do every hour of the day, and how much she expects to accomplish by the time she goes to bed. Maybe I'm envious of her, because too often I just let things happen to me. I react to whatever comes along instead of making things happen. She used to think she was going to join a convent, but lately she's been talking about marriage and motherhood and even a career. By thirty, she says, she wants to be "settled in." Career or marriage or both, she wants to be settled.

No matter how much she tells you, though, you always get the feeling that she's holding back. That you never quite know the real Elizabeth. Maybe everyone's like that to a certain degree. Maybe we never tell our friends everything there is to know about us.

There was no stopping her where Lester was concerned, however. As soon as we got on the bus, Elizabeth told Pamela and Pamela told Brian, and soon everyone knew that we were planning a surprise party for Lester on Saturday.

I didn't get involved. If they wanted to give Lester a cake, it was okay by me. I'd have my hands full just making sure the bathroom was clean and the house straightened up, and helping Dad with the food. That, and algebra.

I was really having trouble with that subject. I worried so much about not understanding it when the teacher wrote things on the board that I concentrated more on the worrying than the problem. But every time I walked in the classroom, my stomach churned.

Whenever I had to put a problem on the board, I could feel perspiration trickling down my sides.

Last year, I would have leaned my head on Patrick's shoulder going home and told him how scared I was, and he would have put his arm around me and volunteered to come over and help me with my homework. But now, if Patrick wasn't staying after school for band practice or something, he was doing extra work in the library for his accelerated programme. I missed him.

"I might as well not even have a boyfriend," I complained to Gwen, the friend who'd helped me with general maths back in year nine. She had a boyfriend, too, and his nickname was Legs. He does athletics every spring with Patrick.

"Yeah? Tell me about it," she joked.

"I never see him! He's always got fifty other things to do!"

"He calls, doesn't he?"

"It's not the same as talking to him in person."

"Well, you can't carry a guy around in your pocket," Gwen said.

"What's that supposed to mean?"

"You've each got to have your own space."

"It's like we've each got a football field of space around us now! What more does he need?" I asked.

She laughed. "A whole city. Some boys need a neighbourhood just to themselves."

I didn't think that applied to Patrick. He'd never said anything about needing more space. He was simply too busy with all he had going on in his life. I should be proud of him, I told myself – somebody as smart and motivated as he was. Most of the time I'd let him decide where we should go and what we should do. He always had the best ideas.

When Gwen and I walked down the corridor together, we had the habit of leaning towards each other, our arms touching. I walk that way with Pamela, too, but Elizabeth doesn't like people leaning on her. Gwen's chocolate-coloured skin against my pinkish-cream made Legs think of sweets, he said – the kind his grandma kept in her sweetie dish.

"If you need help with algebra, I could come over sometime," Gwen offered when we reached the stairwell.

"I don't just need it sometimes, I need it all the time. Every day," I told her. "I don't think I'm going to pass this course."

"You said the same thing about general maths. Don't play dumb on me," Gwen said.

The fact was, I wasn't playing. If a textbook says, *The widest part of North America is from Labrador to British Columbia*, I can see a picture of it in my head. If I read that *The clam has gills that hang into the mantle cavity on each side of the foot*, I know exactly what the book is telling me. I see pictures in my mind. But if I read that *The coefficient is the multiplier of a variable or number, usually written next to the variable*, or [5a+6a={5a-a+7a}-a], I might as well be looking at pigeon tracks in the snow. I can almost feel my eyes roll back and my brain go on hold.

*

"That's life, Al. L-I-F-E. Some things are harder than others," Lester said that evening as we made tacos and salad for dinner. The Melody Inn stays open late on Thursday nights, but it was Janice Sherman's turn to stay at the shop and we wanted to have dinner ready for Dad when he got home.

"Well, life stinks," I said. "I don't want to go through the next four years of school scared to death I'm going to flunk."

"What's the worst that can happen if you do?"

"I'd have to take algebra again next term, which means I'd have to go to summer school for algebra II."

"And . . .?"

"And there are other ways I want to spend my summer!"

"If that's the worst thing that can ever happen to you, be grateful," said my brother, the philosopher, as he sprinkled cheese over the minced beef

"But after algebra, there's geometry, and after geometry, physics!" I cried. "Tell me one single way algebra can help me if I decide to become a psychologist." I had already narrowed my career options to a counsellor or a psychologist rather than psychiatrist, because if I went into psychiatry, I'd have to go to medical school, and if I went to medical school, I'd have to take chemistry and who knows what else.

"Because somewhere along the way, you'll have to take a course in statistics, and you can't enroll in that if you can't pass algebra and geometry, that's why," Lester said.

"Why would I have to take *statistics?*" I bellowed.

Lester handed me the shredder and the lettuce. "Let's say you read a study that most men who commit suicide have sisters. Statistics can help you figure out if the results could have occurred by chance, whether sisters are the actual cause of their brothers' demise, or . . ."

I didn't get to hear the rest, because the phone rang just then and I answered in the hall. It was Aunt Sally in Chicago. She took care of us for a while after Mum died, and I keep mixing up early memories of Mum with her. This sort of freaks Dad out. Aunt Sally calls every so often because she feels responsible for us, I guess. She even flew out for a few days to see how we were doing when Dad was in England.

"So what's new?" asked Aunt Sally.

She used to say, "Alice, how *are* you?" implying that she suspected the worst. But because I often clammed up when she asked that, she's learned to say, "What's new?"

"Well, Dad's on cloud nine," I told her. "I don't know when he and Sylvia are getting married – next July, maybe – but he's really happy these days, and busy as usual at the shop. Lester's back at Uni, and I started school again this week."

"Sounds as though you've all got your work cut out for you," said Aunt Sally. "So what are you doing for fun?"

No matter how she tries to disguise it, whenever Aunt Sally opens her mouth, you know exactly what's eating her. She's not concerned about our work and our studies; she's concerned about what Lester and I are doing for fun, because fun and trouble are never that far apart in Aunt Sally's mind. It's hard to believe that Carol is her daughter, because there's no resemblance between Aunt Sally and my grown-up cousin.

"Well, Les isn't going out with anyone at present. We're celebrating his birthday this Sunday."

"Yes, I've sent him a card. Twenty-two! Can you believe it, Alice? Lester? Twenty-two years old?"

"Yep, I believe it. In fact, he's going to chaperone the mixed pyjama party I'm having here Saturday night," I said.

I don't know why I do that. There's something about me that loves to torture Aunt Sally.

"Alice, ex-*cuse* me, but I thought you said a *mixed* pyjama party!" she gasped.

"That's right. There will be about a dozen of us, if everyone shows."

There was a long pause. Then: "Is your father absolutely, positively out of his mind? Lester, the ultimate playboy, is going to chaperone a dozen hormone-crazed kids on a . . ." She paused again long enough to breathe. "Where are you all going to sleep?"

"On the floor. In sleeping bags. *Individual* sleeping bags," I said, laughing.

"Well, all I can say is that things have certainly changed since I was a girl," Aunt Sally said. "Marie and I couldn't even spend the night with a girlfriend unless Mother knew exactly who would be there. And I would never have considered letting Carol go to a mixed pyjama party. Ever!"

"So she eloped with a sailor," I said, and knew immediately I'd been unfair.

But Aunt Sally just sighed. "Yes, eloped, and divorced two years later." Another pause. "I suppose Patrick will be there?"

"Of course."

"Alice, let me give you one little piece of advice: Familiarity breeds contempt."

"Huh?"

"It's true. The more familiar you let a boy get with you, the more favours you give him, the less respect he will have for you."

Familiar? Favours?

"Then I guess after people marry they absolutely hate each other," I reasoned.

"Oh, I didn't mean that! I just mean there's a lot of truth in the saying that if a girl lets a boy go all the way, he won't respect her in the morning."

"How about halfway?" I teased. I couldn't help myself.

"Now, Alice . . ."

"A third of the way? Three-eighths?"

"Alice . . ."

"Aunt Sally," I said. "Picture this: Twelve guys and girls, each in his or her own sleeping bag, sprawled out on the rug in our living room, with Lester right smack in the middle of us, listening for every sound, watching for any move . . ."

"What *I* see is Lester snoring away, surrounded by a dozen fourteen-year-olds, who . . . well, I've said all I'm going to say on the subject, Alice. But have fun!"

Have *fun?* I knew at least one person I could count on to stay awake Saturday night: Aunt Sally. I always tell Dad he doesn't have to lose any sleep over Lester and me. Aunt Sally will do it for him. I went back out in the kitchen.

"What did Sal have to say?" asked Lester.

"Familiarity breeds contempt," I said.

Lester grinned. "She's got that right," he said. "Every time you wash your undies and drape them over my towel in the bathroom, kiddo, I want to toss you out of the window along with them."

We had dinner ready when Dad got home around six-thirty, and I spent the rest of the evening at the dining room table doing my homework. Lester did the dishes, then went up to his room to read, and Dad sat on the sofa, his feet on the coffee table, a clipboard on his lap, writing to Sylvia Summers.

About nine-thirty, I'd just gone out in the kitchen to get some chocolate digestives when the doorbell rang, and a few moments later I heard Dad's voice in the hallway. "Janice!"

Janice's voice: "I know it's late, Ben, but could I come in for a few minutes?"

"Of course! Something happen at the shop this evening?"

I heard the door close and their feet crossing the hallway into the living room.

"That for me?" Lester yelled from upstairs.

"No, Les. Janice just dropped by," said Dad.

I didn't know what to do. I couldn't very well take my biscuits back into the dining room and sit there chewing while they talked. But if I stayed in the kitchen I'd be eavesdropping. What I should have done was go upstairs, but I didn't.

Dad: "You look upset."

Janice: "I *am* upset. I didn't want to bring this up at the shop, Ben, so I decided to come by and tell you in person. I'll be leaving the Melody Inn at the end of September."

"Janice! Why on earth?"

"I've asked the main office for a transfer, and they'll let me know. I can't go on working for a man I don't trust."

"What? Janice, sit down. Please!"

More footsteps, then a pause. Then the squeak of the sofa springs.

"I've worked for you for six years, Ben. Longer than any of your other employees, and the shop has had its ups and downs. But I thought we made a good team."

"We did, Janice! We do! What do you mean, you don't trust me?"

"I don't expect you to tell me everything that goes on in your life," Janice said, and now her voice was trembling. "But when it's a subject as intimate as marriage, and I have to hear about it from a part-time employee . . ."

"Ah." It was a cross between a sigh and an exclamation, and Dad paused. "Marilyn told you that Sylvia and I are engaged. Right?"

"Can you understand how that made me feel, Ben? Hearing it from her? She gets the news and I don't?"

"Janice, I swear. I know I'm a fool when it comes to social relations sometimes, but it was only because she came right out and asked. I mean, these young women, they just ask these things, so I told her. I didn't think . . . I honestly didn't think you'd be that interested."

Out in the kitchen I clutched my head and closed my eyes. Even I didn't think my dad would say something quite so stupid.

"Y-you didn't think I'd be *interested*? I'm speechless," said Janice.

Dad didn't answer.

"All these years of loving you . . .," she said quietly.

"Janice!"

"And I knew it wasn't reciprocated. I can't blame you for that."

"Janice, I've always been fond of you. You know that."

"'Fond' won't do it, Ben. But I did think you'd have the courtesy – the decency – to let me know first if you became engaged to another woman."

"I was thoughtless and stupid not to tell you first, and I apologise. But is this reason enough for you to leave? Move somewhere else?"

"I think so. I may even make manager at another shop, who knows?"

"Well, if that happens, it will be my great loss and another's gain, Janice. I can only wish you the best of luck, and I mean that sincerely. You'll do a great job wherever you are. I'm just sorry you feel this way."

"So am I, Ben."

I moved my head an inch at a time until I could just see around the doorway into the living room. Janice was getting up from the sofa, her handbag tucked under her arm like a rifle. She walked stiffly across the room towards the front door. I edged back again until I heard my father's footsteps, too, in the hall. Then I peeked again.

"Can I count on you until the end of the month?" he asked.

"Yes. You can count on that," Janice said. "Good-bye, Ben." Suddenly she threw her arms around Dad's neck, her bag dropping to the floor, and pressed her mouth against his. Dad stood as stiff as a broom handle, his palms resting lightly against her waist, but his fingers bent back away from her, afraid, it seemed, to touch her any more than necessary.

Before he could say a word, she turned again, swooped down to pick up her bag, then went out of the front door, closing it behind her.

Dad didn't move.

Les was coming downstairs in his socks. I emerged from the kitchen, and we joined Dad there in the hallway. I didn't know what to say, so I let Les do the talking. He grinned a little ruefully at Dad and said, "Well, Pops, you win some, you lose some."

Dad shook his head. "Can you imagine? And all because Marilyn found out before she did."

But Lester said, "I think it was the only excuse she could come up with. It was only a matter of time before she left. It would have been unbearable for her, once you were married, to have to listen to *Sylvia and I did this*, and *Sylvia and I did that*."

"You're probably right, but I'd no idea she was this unhappy. What am I going to do? Who will I find to replace her? Janice knows the shop almost better than I do. She's a terrific asset!"

"Won't the company send someone else?"

"They always give us a chance to find someone local first."

"Well, the advice you'd give me is to sleep on it, so why don't you?" Lester said.

"I guess I will." But Dad still didn't move; he just stood in the hallway with a dazed look on his face. "Will somebody please explain why the major problems in this household concern romance?" he asked plaintively.

"'Cause love makes the world go around, Dad," I told him.

"And it makes me dizzy," Dad said.

4

The Big Night

There were even more people on Saturday than I'd expected. Kids invited other kids, I guess. The usual crowd was there, the ones who hang out at Mark Stedmeister's pool in the summer: Patrick, Elizabeth and Pamela, Brian and Mark, Karen and Jill, and, lately, Gwen and her boyfriend, Legs. I'd invited two friends from school, Lori Haynes and her friend Leslie, mostly because some of the girls had been so awful to them back in year nine, but I wanted to know Lori better.

Justin Collier came, of course – the guy who likes Elizabeth – but I was surprised when Sam Mayer showed up with his girlfriend, Jennifer. Sam had asked me to the year nine dance last spring, not realising, I guess, that Patrick and I were a couple. That made fifteen people, and Mark had invited Penny, so that was sixteen. Penny's dad actually came to the door to make sure an adult was present. But the biggest surprise of all was that an hour after everyone else had got there, Donald Sheavers rang the doorbell.

Pamela was peering out the window. "It's him!" I heard her squeal, and Elizabeth started laughing.

I looked out. "Who invited *Donald?*" I asked. "*Pamela!*"

"He's cute!" she said.

Donald Sheavers used to be my boyfriend back in years five and six when we were renting a house in Takoma Park. He doesn't even go to our school, and I'd never thought he had much between the ears because he always did whatever I told him. If I'd said, *Donald, jump out the window*, he probably would have jumped. But Pamela met him when we bumped into him at the mall, and then she invited him to the year nine dance, and he'd seemed a lot smarter then.

I wasn't exactly wild to have him at my party though, since he didn't know most of the other kids. Or maybe I remembered the way he always gave a Tarzan yell when he saw me, just because we used to play Tarzan together. Really dumb. It didn't matter where we were – at school, the mall, the playground – whenever Donald saw me, he'd beat his chest and give a Tarzan yell, and it embarrassed me to death.

I opened the door. Donald started beating his chest and opened his mouth, and just as suddenly he closed it again and grinned. "Just kidding," he said.

I laughed and held the door open for him. He had a sleeping bag under one arm. "So where's the party? We all going to sleep in the same bed or what?"

"Shhhh," I said. "Dad's freaking out as it is."

"Don-ald!" Pamela cried dramatically, throwing her arms around his neck, and introducing him to the other kids.

There were already three different card games in progress, but the TV was going, too, and there was the smell of popcorn coming from the kitchen. A car with a Domino's sign on top stopped out front, and a man came to the door carrying five large pizzas.

I guess I'd never seen so many people in our house at one time. Wall-to-wall people. Somebody had a boom box playing softly in one corner, competing with the TV, Karen was snapping Polaroid pictures of everybody, Jill was dancing with Justin Collier and Mark, both at the same time, Penny was strutting around in red flannel pj's with a drop seat, making us all laugh, and Patrick was imitating David Letterman. It was simply loud and fun and busy, just the way a party should be. Donald seemed to fit right in.

Dad wasn't used to cooking for more than four or five people at a time. If we had one other person at the table besides our family, we figured we had a full house. Now Dad couldn't even carry a pizza into the room without stepping over or around bodies – on the floor, in chairs, under chairs, leaning over the back of the sofa.

I guess it was the first time I could remember that I'd had a real party. I mean, more than a few friends in for birthday cake. The first time I'd had music and TV and guys and girls all at the same time. Most definitely the first time I'd ever spent the whole night with guys in the room.

The thing about having a party at your place, though, you feel like you have to be responsible for everybody. You have to keep checking to make sure everyone's having a good time. I was mostly concerned about Lori and Leslie, because I wasn't sure how the other kids felt about them. I noticed that while they stuck pretty close to each other, they didn't hold hands with everyone watching, and certainly didn't kiss. That's the one thing I felt sad about, that Lori and Leslie didn't feel they could be themselves in my home.

The other person I was watching was Elizabeth, mainly to see if she was eating anything. She was doing okay, I guess. I still saw her pause before every bite, as though debating whether she could afford to let herself eat it. But she ate most of a slice of pizza and some grapes and a couple of crisps, which was a lot more than she had allowed herself last summer.

"Penny's wild," Pamela said to me as we passed on the stairs. With only one bathroom, and gallons of Coke and Sprite, people were going up and down all evening.

"What do you mean?"

"Just fun and crazy. Mark's going ape over her."

"Do you care?" I asked, because Pamela used to go out with Mark when she wasn't going out with Brian.

"No way. I'm keeping my options open," Pamela said.

I went back down to the living room. Penny *was* sort of crazy in a fun way. Still wearing those red flannel pj's, she was teaching Donald Sheavers a new dance, and Brian kept trying to get in the act and mess it up. Patrick was sitting on the sofa doing one of his magic tricks for Lori, using Legs as his assistant, while Sam and Jennifer watched TV – Jennifer on his lap.

I slipped out to the kitchen to see if Dad needed any help. He had the harried look of the Old Woman Who Lived in the Shoe, like seventeen homeless kids had just shown up on his doorstep.

"Need anything, Dad?" I asked.

"About three more hands," he said. "I made a big pot of chicken gumbo in case people are still hungry after the pizza, but I thought we had more crackers, and –"

"Oh, Dad, you're wonderful!" I said, and gave him a hug. His eyes lit up like a torch. Every so often it hits me that grown-ups – parents, anyway – need to be told they're doing okay, that they're loved and appreciated. You'd think they wouldn't need that anymore once they're grown, but they do.

Mark had brought a video of one of those old horror movies, *Invasion of the Body Snatchers*, so about ten-thirty we decided to put that on and we all settled down to watch, backs against backs, heads leaning on shoulders, legs over legs, pillows everywhere, till everyone was comfortable. It would have been terrifying if I was watching alone, but Mark and Justin kept making crazy remarks, so we laughed all the while it was on.

At some point I realised the light had gone off in the kitchen and Dad wasn't around anymore. Then I noticed Lester sitting at the back of the room, eating a bowl of gumbo and watching the movie with us.

We clapped and brayed and whistled when the

movie was over, and then the girls discovered that Lester was there and started cosying up to him. It's really amazing to watch. Girls' voices change when they talk to Lester. Their smiles are different. They laugh differently. I caught Lester's eye and made a gagging gesture, and he grinned.

"Hey! Anybody want an egg cream, made by the World's Best Egg Creamer?" Lester said, as much to get Jill and Pamela off the back of his chair as to have something to do, I think.

"What's an egg cream?" asked Brian.

"Ha! Come out to the kitchen and watch a genius at work," Lester said, so everyone traipsed out to the kitchen. He dramatically rolled up his sleeves. "Anybody here who doesn't want one?"

"So what is it?" Pamela asked.

"A drink," said Les.

The guys looked surprised.

"Count me in," said Brian, and everyone wanted to try one, eighteen in all, counting Les.

Lester got out our tall iced-tea glasses, then the water glasses, then a couple of beer steins, and finally a jam jar. He went over to Dad's cupboard and took out the soda water siphon.

After that he took a jar of chocolate-flavoured syrup from the cupboard and a two litre carton of milk from the fridge.

"That's it?" asked Karen.

"Oh, and a spoon. Very important, the spoon!" Lester said, and took one from the drawer. Then, with a flourish, he said, "Observe!"

He carefully spooned an inch of chocolate syrup into the bottom of each glass. When they were all filled, the beer steins and the jam jar, too, he added an inch of whole milk on top of the syrup, going from one glass to the next. Then he took the first glass, tilted it, inserted the spoon and, with his other hand, sprayed the soda water from the siphon directly onto the spoon so that he got a big chocolatey head. He stirred and handed the first glass to Elizabeth.

"Enjoy!" he said.

I don't know what fascinated me most – the way Elizabeth's cheeks turned pink as she took the glass from his hands, or the way the other kids were watching. This was not a treat Elizabeth would ordinarily have allowed herself certainly not last summer, but Lester had chosen her – *her* – to get the first glass. So she lifted it to her lips and drank.

"It's *wonderful!*" she said. And then, as though counting calories, "It's only milk and syrup and soda water?"

"You got it!"

"Where does the egg come in?" asked Penny.

"Search me," said Lester. "It's an old New York drink. Some say it comes from Russia. But is that good or is that good?" He handed the second glass to Penny.

"Ummmm! It's good," she said. And offered Patrick a sip until he got his. I was glad Les served Patrick next.

We migrated back into the living room and sat around savouring the egg creams. There are times I absolutely love my brother. He was the hit of the evening. It was going on one o'clock, and when Les came in with his own egg cream in the jam jar, he said, "Ah, yes! An excellent bedtime drink," hoping we'd take the hint.

"In your dreams," said Pamela.

"We're good for another three hours!" said Justin.

"Besides . . .," Elizabeth added, and looked at Karen and Jill. Suddenly looks travelled all around the room, and Elizabeth and Karen went upstairs to my bedroom and came back down carrying a cake with lighted candles. They'd ordered it from the local bakery, and on the icing, in blue letters, it said, *To Our No. 1 Stud*. The girls started singing "Happy Birthday" and everyone joined in, even the ones who didn't know what it was all about. "Happy birthday to you, happy birthday . . ."

I was sitting on Patrick's lap on the sofa, and we started singing, too. Patrick did, anyway. I never sing "Happy Birthday" because I can't carry a tune.

"Happy birthday, dear Studly . . .," sang Pamela.

As soon as the cake was in Lester's hands, Karen took a picture.

Lester looked a little embarrassed. "Stud?" he said, looking around. "Somebody here named Stud?" Then he laughed.

"Make a wish!" Penny instructed. "Make a wish with all us gorgeous girls around you, and maybe it will come true."

"You mean I can wish this party was over, and you'll all go home?" Lester teased.

"Better than that. Maybe one of us could be your teddy bear for the night," said Pamela.

"Pamela!" Elizabeth scolded. We all laughed again.

"I don't know about that. My old teddy bear had one ear chewed off and an eye missing," Lester said.

"Blow, Lester! The wax is dripping," Gwen told him.

Lester blew out all twenty-two candles, everyone clapped, and then Jill got a knife and cut the cake into twenty pieces. We all dug in.

"Presents! Presents!" cried Pamela. I looked around in surprise. I'd expected the cake, but no one had said anything about presents. I stared as all the girls – all except Leslie and Lori, who hadn't known about it, either – retrieved little packages from their sleeping bags, some flat, some in tiny balls, some in small boxes, and gave them to Lester.

"What's this? What's this?" he asked.

"Open them!" said Elizabeth. "You have to open them in front of everyone."

"Uh-oh," said Lester. "I don't like the sound of that." But he did, and we shrieked as he unwrapped or unrolled, untied or unwound, pair after pair of boxer shorts, each one wilder than the one before. Boxers that looked like newsprint; boxers with ants painted all over them; boxers in a leopard print, boxers with lipstick marks . . .

Les looked around at the girls. "Somebody trying to tell me to change my underwear more often?" he joked.

"No, we want you to model them!" Pamela said, and all the girls laughed.

"Hey, we came empty-handed!" Patrick said.

"No-one told us about presents, Les, but I'll give you the shorts off my bottom if you like."

"No. Thanks, anyway," said Lester.

"How about mine?" said Brian. He stood up and lowered his jeans just enough to show us three inches of bright purple boxer shorts with yellow zigzag lines on them.

"I can top those," said Donald Sheavers, showing off his racing car boxers, and suddenly all the guys were lowering their jeans and all the girls were screeching, and Lester looked relieved when I slipped another movie in the video and eventually everyone turned around to watch.

We weren't ready for sleep, though. Lester went upstairs to put in an half-hour of study while we messed around. Elizabeth and I were gathering up glasses and washing cutlery – stepping over bodies and carrying stuff to the kitchen – when we heard a lot of muffled laughter coming from the next room and I wondered what I was missing. But after all the work Dad had put into the food for the party, I didn't want him to come down the next morning to a sink full of dirty dishes. I went back to the living room for a final check and heard Jill whisper, "There's Alice!" and instantly all heads in the living room jerked towards me with grins on their faces.

"Yeah? What?" I said, laughing.

"Nothing! Nothing!" Brian said.

"Just a little innovative photography," Justin added.

Actually, some of the kids had already staked out spots for their sleeping bags – under the dining room table, beside the sofa, behind my beanbag chair, *on* my beanbag chair. I put in still another video while the girls trooped upstairs in twos and threes to change in my room and brush their teeth. Most of us just took off our jeans and pulled on shorts or sweatpants, but it felt so daring, somehow, to come downstairs with our sleeping bags and put them down next to the boys' on the rug.

There was always a short line outside the bathroom, and the boys were joking about going out in the garden to pee. By the time Lester came back downstairs, almost everyone had found a spot to roll out their sleeping bag, and he went around turning off lights while the movie on the video played on, the volume low.

Patrick had saved a spot for me under the grand piano next to him, so I crawled into my sleeping bag, and he rolled over and kissed me on the mouth.

"Hey! Hey! None of that!" Mark called. "Hey, Les! Over here, man! Sex alert! Sex alert!"

Lester, on the sofa, sleepily raised one eyebrow, gave me a look, and rolled over on his side.

We were all pretty tired. It was almost three o'clock, and I knew that Dad probably hadn't had much sleep yet and was hoping we'd all quieten down. The music, the movie, the food, the warmth of the sleeping bag . . . Patrick and I kissed a while longer, and I was thinking how it would feel if Les wasn't here and we really did both crawl in the same bag. But he fell asleep even before I did, and for most of the night, I slept. So did everyone else, though I woke up briefly around four and was aware that Lester had turned on a table lamp and left it on. I guess he figured that the next best thing to his staying awake all night was the light from a lamp.

I woke again about eight to whispers and giggles, and lifted my head to look around. Lester was sound asleep on the sofa, his mouth agape, snoring peacefully, but Pamela and Jill were slowly, delicately propping cotton buds at odd angles in his thick brown hair.

Other kids began to stir, and when they saw what Jill and Pamela were up to, they began to giggle. Jennifer took some dental floss out of her overnight bag, and Jill unwound it and wrapped it around the cotton buds draping it from stick to stick, turning her head away so she wouldn't breathe or giggle in Lester's face. It looked sort of like a crown. Pamela went out to the kitchen and returned with a sheet of foil. She tore off little pieces and carefully squeezed them over the ends of each cotton bud so that they looked like silver. Both Patrick and I were each sitting up on one elbow now, laughing silently. Karen took a Polaroid picture.

Les gave a sigh and opened his mouth even wider. Penny got in the act and stuck one finger in his mouth. Then she turned to the other kids, most of whom were awake now, all but Donald Sheavers, and mimed that she was going to stick two fingers in without touching the sides of Lester's mouth. Lester snored on. Penny's dimples grew even deeper as she indicated three fingers and gently guided them in without waking Lester. Somebody clapped. This time Penny held up four fingers, but at that moment Lester's mouth snapped shut, and then his eyes opened. He gave a snort, and Penny sat back on her heels.

"Wha'sup?" Lester said groggily. He saw Pamela and Jill and Jennifer all looking at him and laughing. Les swung his legs off the sofa and looked around. As he did so, one of the cotton buds slipped and dangled over his eyes. "What the . . .?" Lester cried, running his hand over his hair. Then he leaped up. "Oh, for crying out loud," he said as the crown fell off, and everyone laughed.

Dad stepped in from the kitchen. "Anybody for waffles and sausage?" he said.

"They're all yours, Dad. I'm outta here," Les said, bolting up the stairs with his blanket and pillow.

Some of the girls went upstairs to shower, two and three crowding into the bathtub at once to save time, a couple of guys went back to sleep, but by ten, half of us had eaten Dad's waffles and the other half were getting dressed. A few kids, Patrick included, had already gone home, and the rest drifted away, one by one, most of them telling me that they'd had a really great time, and I knew they meant it. You can just tell.

When the last person had gone, I went out in the kitchen to help with the dishes. Dad looked at me. I looked at him.

"Whew!" he said, and we both laughed.

"Thanks, Dad," I told him. "Everyone had a really great time. And there wasn't any sex going on, if that's what you're going to ask me next."

"I wasn't, but I'm glad to hear it," he said.

I spent the next hour putting the house back in shape, running the hoover over the rug and the dining room, cleaning the popcorn off the sofa and chairs, rearranging the furniture, carrying more glasses to the kitchen. There were Polaroid pictures all over the top of the piano, and I got myself a glass of orange juice and sat down on the sofa to enjoy them.

There was a photo of Brian eating a piece of pizza; Elizabeth carrying the birthday cake; Lori and Mark and Jill and Justin playing cards; Gwen and Legs watching the movie; me with my mouth open, eating popcorn; Lester holding up a pair of boxer shorts; Lester on the sofa with cotton buds in his hair, and then . . . I suddenly felt like a block of ice without any heartbeat at all. Because there in my hand was a picture of Patrick and Penny with their arms around each other, kissing.

5

That Sinking Feeling

I couldn't breathe for a moment, and then I sank down on the sofa, not taking my eyes from the picture.

On this sofa, this very sofa where I was sitting, Penny and Patrick were turned towards each other in the photo. She had one hand on his shoulder, he had a hand on her waist, and their faces were turned at an angle so you could see most of the back of Patrick's head and one side of Penny's face.

How *could* they? How could *he?*

My eyes were brimming over, and tears spilled down my cheeks. I felt humiliated, angry, and lost. How could they do this in my very own house? Here at my *party?* Why had Karen taken their picture? And then I remembered when I'd walked in the living room once and heard someone whisper, "There's Alice," as though a secret was travelling around the place. Everyone was in on it but me.

I leaned back against the sofa cushions, covered my face with my hands, and sobbed. Maybe Karen had left it behind just so I'd find out. Maybe Patrick had been seeing Penny for weeks and no-one had the nerve to tell me.

The phone rang, but I didn't want to answer. Lester was still sleeping, though, and Dad was outside raking leaves. So I got up, swallowed, and walked to the phone in the hall.

"Hello?" I said, but it didn't sound like me.

There was a pause.

"Al?" Pamela's starting to mimic Lester now, calling me "Al."

"Yeah? What do you want?" I said hoarsely.

"My gosh, it doesn't sound like you at all. I think I left my sweater at your place. I'm on my way over to pick it up, okay?"

"All right."

Another pause. "You sound like you've been crying."

I swallowed again.

"Alice, have you been crying?" she asked.

"Pamela!" I bawled. I couldn't hold back any longer.

"What's the matter? What's *happened?*" And then, before I could say anything, she said, "You saw the picture, I'll bet."

Everybody knew, then! Everyone was waiting. All the kids knew that Patrick was falling for Penny, and no-one knew how to tell me, least of all Patrick.

"I'll be right over," Pamela said, and hung up.

I sat down on the stairs, too weak to do anything else. Yesterday had been so wonderful. I'd felt attractive and popular and clever and fun. Now I felt like old news, yesterday's left-overs. I felt tricked and pitied.

I knew I should go and wash my face before Pamela got here, but I couldn't even make myself do that. Now that she said she was coming, I wanted her to hurry up and get here. I wanted to know how long she'd known Patrick was cheating on me and how many of the other kids knew.

When her footsteps sounded on the porch, I heard voices and realised that Elizabeth was with her. They'd come together to let me know that Patrick was breaking up with me, to be with me in my time of need. I didn't *want* to be pitied. I didn't *want* to be sad. Yet here I was, and the minute I opened the door, I started crying again.

Instantly Elizabeth put her arms around me, but Pamela was saying, "Al, it was a joke! That's all it was, just a joke."

"Well, if th-that was a joke, I don't get it," I sobbed. "How long have you known something was going on?"

"I didn't know anything until Pamela came over and got me and said you were upset about a picture," said Elizabeth. "*What* picture?"

We were an odd-looking lot. Elizabeth had obviously just got home from Mass, because she was wearing a dark green dress. Pamela had changed to shorts, even though it was only sixteen degrees out, and I was still dressed in the clothes I'd worn yesterday. Wordlessly I led them into the living room and handed Elizabeth the photo.

She stared at it, then at Pamela. "Where was I when they took this picture?" she asked.

"I don't know. You and Alice were off in the kitchen somewhere, and Karen was just being . . . well, Karen. She was telling us how you could make pictures lie so it looked like something was happening that wasn't, and she'd seen someone take a picture at a party where it looked like a couple was kissing when they weren't, and Penny said, 'Let's try it!' and chose Patrick. It was supposed to be *a joke*, Alice!"

Pamela was calling me Alice again, so I knew she was serious. But the words "chose Patrick" rang in my ears. Why not Mark or Brian or Donald or Justin? Why did she choose a guy who was actually going out with someone? And then, the question that hurt even more, why had Patrick agreed to do it?

"Look!" Pamela explained. "They weren't even touching. I helped arrange them."

"*You?*" I cried.

Pamela looked chagrined. "Well, if they're going to do it, wouldn't you rather have one of your friends calling the shots to be sure it's legit? We had them arranged so that their lips were two inches apart, their hands weren't touching each other, but from across the room, in the camera, it looked like a real kiss."

"That's a scream," I wept. "I never saw anything so funny in my life."

"Forgive and forget," Elizabeth said quickly, trying to be helpful.

When Pamela went upstairs to get her sweater, Elizabeth said, "Patrick probably couldn't help himself

All the guys are nuts about Penny. It's just hormones, that's all it is."

That was supposed to make me feel better?

When Pamela came back down, we went out to sit in the sunshine on the front steps. We could hear the quiet *scrape*, *scrape* of Dad's rake at the side of the house.

"This was supposed to be a beautiful September," I said ruefully. "I wanted it to be an autumn I'd always remember – year ten. I'll remember it, all right."

"Seventy times seven," said Elizabeth.

"What? What are we doing now, the multiplication tables?"

"That's how many times you're supposed to forgive someone."

"Great!" I said. "Patrick gets to kiss her four hundred and ninety times more." I guess I'm pretty good at arithmetic when it's important.

"He didn't *kiss* her!" Pamela insisted.

No, he hadn't kissed her, but he'd been two inches away from her lips, I thought. He had smelled the scent of her hair, looked into her eyes . . . If he hadn't kissed her, I'll bet he'd wanted to.

I leaned back on my elbows. "She's like a magnet," I said. "What is it about small, petite girls, anyway? The boys go crazy over them, and it makes the rest of us feel like elephants."

"I don't feel like an elephant. You're exaggerating," said Pamela. "And you have to admit she's a lot of fun. You'd better take it as a joke, Al, because everyone else is."

"I know. I'm making a mountain out of a molehill. I guess I just wanted it to be the perfect party, and this was the part that wasn't so perfect," I said.

"I've got to go have lunch," said Elizabeth. "I'll see you later, guys."

We watched her cross the street.

"I have to go, too," said Pamela. "Dad's taking me to a baseball game."

I glanced over at her. "Sounds like you're getting along better!"

"We're making 'a conscious effort,' as Dad puts it. Anyway, it'll get me out of the house when Mum calls. She always calls on Sunday afternoons, and I don't much feel like talking to her. Then I've got a ton of homework to do."

"Me, too," I told her. I'd thought the homework last year was awful, but it was nothing like what they give you in year ten.

I sat on the porch a while longer and let the sun warm my legs as Pamela went back down the street. Finally I heard Lester in the kitchen, making something gross in the blender, so I went back inside. He was pouring some kind of skimmed milk/banana/oatmeal mixture into a glass, and he seemed only half awake.

"Shut up," he said, before I even opened my mouth.

"Happy birthday, dear Les-ter . . .," I warbled off-key.

"Oh, geez, don't ruin it," he said.

"I just wanted you to know that Dad and I are

taking you out to dinner tonight, and as my present to you, I'm doing all the dishes this week, even though you're on kitchen duty."

That perked him up a little. "My laundry, too?"

"Don't push it," I said. I watched him glug down the concoction; then stick a crumpet in the toaster. He was wearing an old pair of boxer shorts with lemons on them, and a ripped T-shirt.

I felt like crying again, but I didn't. "Lester," I said. "If there was this girl you had really, really liked for a long time –"

"Don't start," he said.

"No, I need to know. And let's say there was this party and all your friends were there, and it was going on all night, everybody having a good time . . ."

Lester reached into the fridge and took out the butter.

". . . and the next morning you found a Polaroid picture somebody had taken of" – I didn't want to say "kissing" because Lester probably wouldn't be bothered by a kiss – "of this girl lying naked on the sofa with a naked guy on top of her, and –"

"What?" Lester yelled, dropping the butter.

". . . and you found out it was all trick photography to make them *look* like they were having sex, but they weren't, would . . .?"

Lester grabbed me by one arm. "Who was it? Pamela? Jill?"

I shook my head. "Nobody."

"Al, did anyone get naked last night while I was sleeping?"

"No."

"Did anyone have sex with their clothes *on?*"

"No."

"Then will you please get out of my face and let me enjoy my breakfast in peace?"

"Lester, really! I need your advice!" I said, sitting down across from him, and told him about the photo of Patrick and Penny.

"So if it's all a joke, what's the big deal?" he asked.

"It *hurts*, Lester!"

"Maybe so, but the best thing you can do is laugh and forget it."

"I can't."

"Okay, then. Get on the bus tomorrow and claw Patrick's eyes out. That'll really endear you to him. C'mon, Al. Snap out of it."

"I guess you're right," I said, and went upstairs.

For a while I managed to put the picture out of my mind, and worked on some history homework. I went back down around two and ate part of a sandwich Dad had left and some pretzels, but when I started to go up again and saw the sofa where Patrick had been sitting with Penny, where everyone had been whispering, it started the feelings all over again.

I lay for a long time on my bed staring up at the ceiling, at the cobweb that was strung between my light fixture and the wall. It was beginning to collect dust, and looked like a cable on the Brooklyn Bridge. Was Karen trying to start a fight between Patrick and me? I wondered. Was Penny trying to come between us?

I heard the doorbell ring. Lester's footsteps in the downstairs hall.

"Hey, Al! It's Patrick," he called.

Patrick! For a moment I didn't move. I wouldn't go down. I *couldn't!* Then I realised how weird it would seem if I didn't. I leaped up and yelled, "Be down in a sec." I brushed my teeth and put on a little eye make-up so my eyes wouldn't look puffy, then went downstairs. My smile felt about as false as Jill's eye-lashes or Karen's fingernails.

"Hi," I said. Even my voice sounded fake. It sounded as though it came from the tiny chest of a Barbie doll.

"Hi," said Patrick. "Want to walk over to the school or something? Get some ice-cream?"

The school is the lower school nearby, where our gang still gathers sometimes. We sit on the rubber swings, talking to each other, whirling the swings around, scaring all the little kids away.

"Well, I'm not sure," I said. "I'm sort of busy. We're taking Lester out to dinner tonight, and I've got all this homework."

"So have I, but I've been at it all morning. Need a break," he said. A lock of red hair hung down over the left side of Patrick's forehead, and he seemed to have grown another two inches since the day before. He playfully jiggled my arm. "C'mon. It'll do you good."

"Okay," I said.

We went outside. Dad was still at it, transplanting azalea bushes. He always seemed to be tinkering with the garden or the house since he came back from England. Getting things ready for Miss Summers, of course.

"Going for a walk, Dad," I called.

He waved and bent over the azaleas again. Patrick and I started our typical slow walk down the street, his arm around my waist, but it didn't seem like old times anymore. Usually I lean against him in an easy, comfortable manner, but this time my body resisted, and I discovered I was walking with my arms folded in front of my chest, as though I were cold.

Patrick looked down at me. "My, aren't we friendly!" he said.

I managed a smile. "Sorry. Got homework on my mind," I lied.

"Algebra?"

"That's later. I haven't even started it yet."

"Want me to stick around and help?"

"No, I'll manage. Lester's here if I've got any questions."

We walked a little further. "Great party last night," Patrick said. "Everyone had a good time."

"Evidently." Why is it that even when you *know* what not to say, you end up saying it?

Patrick gave my waist a little tug. "What's the matter with you, anyway?"

There was no use in pretending. "I found a photo of you and Penny, Patrick. That's what's the matter."

"Didn't anyone explain about that picture?" he asked, with not a trace of guilt.

"Well, you certainly didn't."

"It was all a pose, Alice! We weren't even touching! We were just horsing around for laughs."

"Ho-ho-ho."

"Karen was going to show it to you, and then you put in another video and I guess we just forgot."

"And it didn't occur to you to tell me about it?"

"I *forgot* about it! Why are you getting so upset?"

I felt stupid and silly, yet still betrayed. "I don't know. How would you feel if after a party at your place, you found a picture of me kissing Justin or Donald Sheavers?"

"We weren't kissing!"

"I know it, but –"

"If I found a picture like that, I'd probably pick up the phone and ask you about it."

"So I'm asking. How come Penny picked you?"

"I don't know. I just went along for the ride." Patrick let his arm drop, and a space developed between us there on the street. "What is this? The third degree? We were just having fun. Isn't that allowed?"

I felt awful then. Deserted. "Of course, Patrick! It's just that everyone seems so secretive about it, as though there's something between you and Penny I'm not supposed to know about."

"There's nothing secret. She's just fun, that's all." And when I didn't answer, he said, "Hey! She's not you, Alice."

"I wonder why that doesn't help." I knew I shouldn't have said that.

Patrick thrust his hands in his pockets, and we

walked a few minutes in silence. The *thrub* of my heart seemed to echo in my ears.

"We're not married, you know," Patrick said finally, without smiling. "I think I'm still allowed to have friends."

"Of course you are," I said, beginning to regret the whole conversation. "I guess I'm acting dumb about it."

I thought he'd put his arm around me then, glad to be forgiven, but he didn't.

"I . . . I don't want you to think you have to have my permission every time you want to talk to another girl," I added.

He didn't answer for a while. We just walked on slowly, a foot apart, but finally he moved closer and then he put one arm around my shoulder. "I'm going to be leaving school a year before you," he said. "I'll be away at college. I'll meet new people, and so will you. We've both got to be free to make friends, Alice."

I could feel tears gathering behind my eyelids, but I managed to hold them back. "I know," I said. And then, trying to be funny, I added, "but remember our date for New Year's Eve when we're both twenty-one. You'll call me, you said."

He just laughed. "I'll put it on the calendar," he promised.

6

Moving On

When I got on the bus the next morning, Patrick was sitting with the guys in the last row, and Penny was up on her knees, leaning over the back of the seat, talking to Jill and Karen.

"Hi, everybody!" I said, my smile moulded onto my face as though set in concrete.

"Hey, Al! Great party!" Mark called.

Some of the girls turned then, Penny included.

"Yeah, we had a great time!" said Jill.

"Lester's so *funny!*" said Penny.

"Was he wearing any of the shorts we gave him?" Karen asked.

I managed a laugh. "I don't keep track of his underwear," I said.

The kids from the other years cast us curious glances, and Elizabeth giggled. Penny and Jill and Karen laughed, too. Then it was like we were all friends again, and Penny pulled me down on the seat next to her to see the little rosebud tattoo she got on her wrist, non-permanent, of course, and Elizabeth squeezed in beside us.

"I've got this friend who has a tattoo on her bum,"

said Karen. "Permanent! She'll never get it off!"

"What kind is it?" Elizabeth wanted to know.

"Popeye! Can you imagine?"

"Can you imagine lying naked while a man tattoos you?" asked Elizabeth.

"Hey, that would be the best part!" said Penny, and we laughed some more. An older girl in front of us glanced around with a bemused expression, and that set us off again.

"Hey, Alice, did you find the picture Karen took?" asked Jill.

I didn't miss a beat. "Yeah, Patrick told me about it. The artificial kiss," I said, and couldn't believe how natural I sounded. How comfortable and confident and easy.

"We were just acting up," Penny said. "I always get nutty around friends."

How did I know I wouldn't like this girl? I thought. How did I know she might not become one of my best friends? I felt one hundred percent better by the time we got to school. Two hundred percent better when Patrick came up behind me as we were getting off and slipped his hands around my waist, kissing me on the side of my neck. I nuzzled him in return. Everything was back to normal. I felt loved and secure.

The drama club met for the first time after school. Mostly we just sat around talking, the drama coach, Mr Ellis, outlining his plans for the spring production, telling us some of the plays he was considering, as though we had a vote in the matter.

Pamela was the only person there I knew. She fit right in with that blue streak in her hair, because a lot of the kids wore black, with black make-up and purple lips and hair. But when one of the purple-lipped girls asked a question, she sounded intelligent. Even nice. Maybe my world was broadening, I thought. Maybe I could learn to get along with girls I was jealous of, and people who looked and dressed like they lived on another planet.

"Just so I can get some idea of what we have here to work with, how many of you are interested in acting, and how many are here for stage crew?" Mr Ellis asked. "Let's see a show of hands for actors."

Most of the kids, Pamela included, wanted to act.

"When it's time to do casting, we have to open it to the whole school, of course, so there are no guarantees," Mr Ellis said, "but I've found that the bulk of the major roles each year go to members of the drama club. Now, how about stage crew – set design, costumes, props, lighting – that kind of thing. Everyone else here for that?"

The rest of us raised our hands. There was only one other girl besides myself, I discovered, who wanted to be part of the crew. She was short and squat, dressed in overalls. Her hair was light brown – modified punk – and she had huge blue eyes. We gave each other sympathetic smiles when we realised all the rest of the crew were guys.

"Anyone here for something *other* than acting or stage crew?" Mr Ellis asked, smiling. "Simple curiosity, maybe?"

A guy sitting to one side, dressed completely in black and purple, raised his hand. "Director," he joked, and we all laughed.

"Looks like we'll be seeing a lot of each other," the blue-eyed girl said when the session was over. "I'm Molly."

"I'm Alice," I said.

It felt good to be branching out – to feel myself *stretch*. Patrick wasn't the only one who had extra things to do and places to go after school.

At home, we could hardly keep up with Dad. All week long he had been relandscaping the whole garden, front and back, putting a dogwood tree in one place, a red maple in another, azaleas on both sides of the front steps, rhododendron, tiger lilies, ivy, a magnolia . . .

"How do you know Sylvia will like all this stuff?" I asked him as he came in with muddy work gloves to get a drink of water.

"Because I've chosen all her favourite plants and trees," he said.

"Are we going to keep living here, then, after you're married?"

"We've talked about it," Dad said. "She loves her own little place, but it's just too small for the four of us, so it makes sense that she moves here." Dad smiled at the thought of it. "She'll certainly make the house a home, with all her little touches."

"It's already a home," I said, somewhat resentfully.

Dad looked over at me from the sink. "Of course it

is, honey. But won't it be nice to have a mum around?"

"You know how much I've wanted this, Dad, but she's really not my mother. I don't think I can ever call her that."

"You don't have to. 'Sylvia' will do."

I continued nibbling a carrot. "Are you going to visit her again before she comes back in June?" I asked.

"I'd like to. We'll have to see."

"Christmas?"

"Not Christmas. That's our busiest time at the store, and I won't have Janice this year, remember. Besides, Sylvia plans to do a little travelling over the holidays, see a bit more of the country before her year is up."

How could two people in love stay away from each other that long? I wondered. A lot could happen in eight months.

It was my turn to make dinner, and I was having hamburgers, oven-made French fries, and a salad. As I scrubbed the potatoes and cut them in long strips, I tried to imagine another person living in our house. Dad's bedroom is the largest. He has two huge wardrobes on either side of a bay window. There are clothes poles in only one of them, though. The other has built-in drawers at the back for blankets and stuff, and shelves along the sides, so I don't know where Sylvia's clothes would go. And we only have one bathroom. That could be a problem. It's *already* a problem!

I sprinkled the potato slices with olive oil and salt

and stuck them in the oven while I looked around the kitchen, trying to see it through Sylvia's eyes.

It's a big, old-fashioned kitchen with lots of cupboards, but little counter space. We have a large dining room, a large living room and a full basement. Dad uses a corner of our dining room for his office, but all that will change when he marries Sylvia, he says, because she'll need an office, too.

"I'm thinking of finishing the basement," Dad, said at dinner. "Insulation, panelling, wall-to-wall carpet . . . I want Sylvia to have plenty of room for her school things, and I could use a real honest-to-goodness desk. If I turned half of the basement into office space, would that be okay with you two?"

I dipped one of my French fries into a pool of ketchup and thought about Miss Summers's house, the few times I'd been in it. I know how she liked having her desk by the back window overlooking the garden and bird feeder.

"How do you know she'll like working in a basement?" I asked.

"It's all we've got," Dad said simply. "But she can hang plants all over the place if she likes. Decorate the house any way she wants."

"Not my room!" I said. "I want my room exactly the way it is now." I guess you could call it jungle decor – the bedspread, the chair, the large rubber plant in one corner . . .

"I'm sure Sylvia isn't going to touch your room, Al. Or yours, either, Les. You can keep your rooms the way you want them."

"Seems to me the solution would be for me to get an apartment somewhere and let you and Sylvia use my room as an office," he said. "I've sponged off you long enough, Dad."

"For one thing, Sylvia wouldn't hear of it," Dad told him. "And for another, it saves us a lot of money, your living at home. Until you're out of college, Les, money's going to be tight, and we enjoy having you around."

"For what? The court jester?" Lester said. "If I could share an apartment with a bunch of guys, it might not be so expensive."

"Les, you are free to do whatever you want. But I think Sylvia would be very distressed if you moved out on her account. Why don't you live at home for at least another year while we all get acclimatised to one another, become a family, and later, if you want to live somewhere else, you can make the decision then."

Somehow I'd never thought of Lester leaving home. Oh, if he married, of course. But living single somewhere else? Away from Dad and me? I wanted change, and I didn't. Looked forward to it and dreaded it both at the same time.

I was over at Elizabeth's when she and her mum had this argument. I've almost never heard of Liz and her mum arguing at all, and especially not in front of other people. She and I were sitting on the sofa looking through a magazine and her mother had just put Nathan down for his nap.

Mrs Price stopped in the doorway of the living room and said, "Did you get my note about your piano lesson? You said you couldn't make it Friday, so he's going to squeeze you in Saturday at one forty-five."

"I already called him and cancelled," Elizabeth said, turning the page again to an article titled, "Does He Want You for Your Mind or Your Body?"

Mrs Price was carrying an armload of Nathan's clothes to the basement, and she leaned against the door frame. "*What?*"

"I cancelled. I've got a big assignment to write this weekend."

"Elizabeth Ann, all you said was that you couldn't do it Friday, and Mr Hedges has gone out of his way to move appointments around so he could take you."

"Well, he'll just have to move them back again. You never told me you were making it Saturday," said Elizabeth.

I pretended to be engrossed in men who want you for your mind, but I was right in the line of fire between Elizabeth and her mum.

"Why didn't you *say* you didn't want a lesson at all this weekend?" Mrs Price asked in exasperation. "We are so lucky that Mr Hedges accepted you at all, and now, after he's taken an interest in your playing, this seems so ungrateful."

"Well, I'm not having a lesson this weekend, Mother, and I've taken care of it," Elizabeth said, and I noticed her voice was shaking.

"I just wish you'd told me earlier," her mother snapped, and went on down to the basement.

Elizabeth didn't say any more, but I could see she was upset, and I went home shortly after that.

When I went to the Melody Inn the following Saturday to put in my three hours of work, I discovered that Janice Sherman was leaving sooner than she had expected. She had an offer to manage a Melody Inn in Toledo, Ohio, and wanted to go early to find a place to live. Dad said she could, that we'd make do somehow till he got a replacement. Everybody was being ultrapolite and friendly to her, and she was being her usual methodical self, putting Post-it notes on every shelf in her office, on every box and drawer, saying exactly where everything was so we wouldn't go bananas after she left.

"When did all this happen?" Marilyn whispered to me when I dusted the shelves in the Gift Shoppe, the little boutique under the stairs leading to the practice cubicles above. "Did she and your dad have a fight or something?"

I didn't want to say more than I should, so I just told her, "No, I think Janice figures it's time she moved on."

But Marilyn didn't buy it. "Move out, is more like it. Your dad comes back from England with the news that he and Sylvia Summers are engaged, and suddenly Janice Sherman is looking for a new place to work. We all know she's nuts about him." When I didn't answer, she asked, "Who's he going to get to replace her?"

"I don't know," I answered. "I suppose he'll advertise. Or maybe headquarters will send a replacement."

All day long the instructors stopped by Janice's office and stood in her doorway with their cups of coffee, making small talk, saying how they'd miss her, asking about the store in Toledo.

"I think living in Ohio will be a nice change of pace," she'd say.

I guess almost any place can be nice, but I don't think I would give up a job near Washington, D.C., for Toledo. Still, she seemed genuinely pleased that the instructors thought enough of her to ask, and Dad took her out to lunch.

When they got back, Marilyn and I had decorated Janice's office with goodbye balloons. We'd all chipped in to buy her a jacket from the shop next door, a red jacket that she'd mentioned to Marilyn she liked. I'd gone across the street for brownies and grapes, and Janice was delighted by the fuss we were making over her. I had to admire her for looking so cheerful when I knew she was leaving because it was hopeless to stick around a man who was in love with another woman.

Would I keep hanging around a guy who was in love with someone else? I wondered. Why did life have to be so complicated? Dad was in love with Miss Summers, but for a while she'd been in love with Jim Sorringer. Janice Sherman was in love with Dad, who didn't love her back. Marilyn was still in love with Lester, who wasn't in love with anyone at the moment. Wouldn't it be simpler if we were just assigned somebody when we reached the age of twenty-five? Maybe there was something to the custom of arranged marriages after all.

Marilyn and Dad took turns darting in and out of Janice's office to wait on customers, then they'd come back, and we all watched while Janice tried on the red jacket. The instructors stopped in between students for a cup of coffee and a brownie, but by two o'clock, it was past time for me to go.

"Goodbye, Janice," I said. "I hope you'll be really, really happy in Toledo." If only I'd stopped there. Why didn't I just say, "We'll probably hear that the Toledo branch is leading all the others in sales, once you take over," or something. Instead, I said, "Next thing you know, we'll probably hear that you're married."

There was a three-second silence, but it seemed like three minutes to me. Everyone stared at me, then they all started talking at once, cleaning up cups, taking another grape, and Janice said, "I'm not going to Ohio to look for a husband, Alice; I'm going for the job."

I blushed and tried to avoid Dad's withering stare. "Of course! I just mean, that'll probably happen, too! I mean . . ." I tried to laugh it off. "You in that red jacket, well . . . Wow!"

"She does look great in it," one of the instructors said.

But Dad said, "If you hurry, Al, you can still make the two-twenty bus."

I gave Janice a quick hug and left the shop, my

cheeks burning. Why don't I think before I open my mouth? And yet, was it really so terrible?

Lester got home before Dad. He works at a men's shoe shop at weekends – an upmarket one, he says, where all the customers wear navy-blue dress socks up to their knees, and have tassels on their Italian-made loafers.

"We had a going-away party for Janice at the shop today and I blew it," I told him.

Lester took off his jacket and dropped it on a chair. "What'd you do? Sneeze in the punch?"

I told him what I'd said about her marrying. "Why couldn't she take it as a compliment?" I asked, following him out to the fridge, where he stood taking things out one at a time, sniffing them, then setting them on the table. "We'd just given her a red jacket that made her look young and pretty, and everyone knows she's been disappointed in love, and –"

"That's exactly why you don't say something like that. Besides, aren't you doing a little stereotyping here? Janice can only be happy if she gets a man? You don't have to be part of a couple to be happy, you know."

"But look how happy Dad's been since he met Miss Summers!"

"He was missing Mum, of course. But you can be part of a couple and still be miserable. Or be single and happy. I'm not part of a couple at the moment, and I'm a heck of a lot happier than I was dating Eva Mecuri."

I thought of Lester's last girlfriend, and had to agree on that.

Six o'clock came, and Dad wasn't home, then six-thirty. Lester and I made cheese omelettes for ourselves and left the egg and cheese and chive mixture in the fridge for Dad.

"Maybe he took Janice out to dinner, too," I said. "Maybe she became hysterical at the thought of never seeing him again, and –"

"Don't!" Lester said, and turned on the TV.

Six-thirty became seven . . . then seven-fifteen . . . seven-thirty. I began to get worried. I called the Melody Inn, but no-one answered.

At a quarter of eight, Dad pulled into the drive, and when he came in he apologised. "I should have called," he said. "Sorry. Hope you two weren't worried."

Lester turned off the TV. "We only called all the hospitals, the state police, and the army," he told him.

"Did Janice Sherman change her mind about leaving?" I asked.

"No. I thought she was rather pleased with all the attention. *Loved* the red jacket. I think things are rather good between us, actually. No hard feelings."

"Then where . . .?" I asked, and waited.

"A surprising new development," Dad said. "Actually, I took Marilyn Rawley to dinner."

One of Lester's feet slid off the coffee table, and he stared at Dad. Marilyn Rawley was an old girlfriend of Lester's – the first *serious* girlfriend, in fact, who had ever come to our house. She was "country" through and through – a sort of '60s flower child, with long straight brown hair. She was small and thin – the kind you could see walking barefoot through a meadow in a see-through cotton dress and no bra. A lot different from Crystal, with her short red hair and big breasts and her classical taste in music. But I'd liked Crystal, too!

"Yeah?" was all Lester said, but his eyes were fixed on Dad.

"As soon as Janice had left the shop and Marilyn and I were cleaning up, Marilyn said to me point-blank, 'Mr McKinley, I'd like to be considered for Janice's position.' Just like that."

"Really?" I cried.

"She's in *college!*" said Lester "She's working on her degree."

"I know," said Dad. "I told her I needed someone full time to be assistant manager, and she said she was willing to drop her courses in order to get the job. I said I didn't think that was a good idea, but she told me she was on the verge of dropping out, anyway, that college wasn't where she wanted to be."

"You're not going to let her, are you?" asked Les.

"I wasn't, but it turns out she had already talked to her adviser about leaving school. She said she was dropping out whether she got the position or not. So I suggested we talk about it more over dinner, and we went to that little Chinese place just off Georgia Avenue, and . . . to make a long story short . . . over beef and green peppers . . . I hired her."

Lester frowned, but I was delighted. "Great!" I said. I could see us now – one big, happy family: Dad and Sylvia, Lester and Marilyn, me and . . .

"She's good with customers, Les, and she does know music – classical as well as folk and rock. I suggested a three-month trial period – see how she likes the business end of it, shuffling papers . . . If it doesn't work out, she can be a sales assistant full time and I'll hire someone else for assistant manager. What do you think?"

"*I* think it's a great idea!" I said.

"Maybe so," said Lester. "She's been less than motivated about getting a degree."

"Soooo," Dad said, relief in his voice. "Nice to have *that* settled. I guess today was a day of moving onward for Janice and upward for Marilyn."

I watched him hang his suit coat in the cupboard. "How was the final goodbye with Janice Sherman?" I asked.

"Cordial," said Dad.

"Cordial?" I teased. "Was there a kiss in that cordial?"

"Actually, yes. And a hug as well."

"On the lips or on the cheek?" I quizzed.

Dad laughed. "On the ear, as I remember. The kind that shows you're not too serious. But Janice did a lot for the Melody Inn, Al. Don't knock it."

"I won't, but Marilyn will do so much more!" I said.

"We'll see," said Dad.

*

I was glad he didn't yell at me for what I'd said to Janice about getting married. But I wondered if having Marilyn at the shop full time would bring her and Lester together again.

It would be the best of all possible worlds for me, I thought. Elegant Sylvia Summers in her beautiful, soft clothes and wonderful perfume, and Marilyn Rawley in her cotton dresses and bare feet. What one couldn't teach me about life, the other could. If Lester would only fall in love with Marilyn again, and marry her, Marilyn and I would be sisters-in law, and she and Lester could have four children, all playing barefoot in the grass and wearing flowers in their hair and playing guitars and singing folk songs, and . . .

The phone rang, and I picked it up in the hall.

"Alice!" came Pamela's voice. "Are you going?"

"Going where?"

"Penny's Halloween party. Didn't she call you?"

There was that cold, sliding-down feeling again. "No . . ."

"Well, she will, I'm sure. At her house on Halloween. Costumes and everything. Elizabeth and I are going. All the guys have been invited, Brian told me."

My lips seemed to stick together. "Did you get . . . invitations in the post, or what?"

"No. She called. Oh, you're invited, I know."

We talked for a few minutes, and then I made an excuse to go. I didn't want to tie up the phone.

But eight became nine, nine-fifteen, nine-thirty . . .

I checked a few times to make sure no-one was using the phone. It sat silently in the hallway, its buttons like little square eyes, mocking me. Twice I checked my E-mail. No message from Penny there, either.

And then, about a quarter of ten, Penny called. "Hi, Alice. I wanted to be sure you knew about my party," she said, and told me the date and the time.

"Sure," I said. "Sounds great." But I couldn't help feeling she'd saved me till last, that I was at the very bottom of her list.

7

Panic

Things were going to be all right. Penny was just what everyone said she was – cute as a penny, funny, friendly, and open, and it was okay that all the boys, Patrick included, liked her. How could they not? Just because Patrick liked her didn't mean he liked me less, or that I wasn't special to him.

I didn't want an ugly costume, though. Penny was also pretty and petite, and I wasn't about to go as a clown or something, with a big nose. I decided to go as a flapper, one of those 1920s girls in the short fringed skirt and headband. I told Pamela and Elizabeth, and we all decided to be flappers together. Mrs Price said she'd help with the costumes, and we had a lot of fun getting the stuff together and trying it on.

"We've got to have plumes in our headbands!" Pamela said one afternoon, lifting some stuff out of a shopping bag. "I stopped at the fabric shop and found the wildest stuff!"

I squealed as she handed me a green feather plume to stick in the sequined headband I'd be wearing, which matched the short, swishy dress Mrs

Price had made for me. It was rectangular, all one piece, no waist, with a fringe of the same colour around the hem.

"And a garter!" Elizabeth said. "We've each got to have a garter. Pastel tights and a garter."

Mrs Price had as much fun as any of us. We had to take turns watching Elizabeth's baby brother while her mum sewed the dresses on her machine. We tickled Nathan with our plumes while he crawled around the floor, trying to get away from us and giggling.

My dress was pale green, Elizabeth's was red, and Pamela's was purple, which made the blue streak in her hair stand out all the more. I bought the matching tights for all of us, and an hour before the party Saturday night, Pamela and Elizabeth came over to show our costumes to Dad and Lester.

Lester was getting ready to go down to Georgetown with some friends, where all the college kids gather on Halloween. At the moment, though, he was sitting on the sofa reading *Newsweek* and eating an apple. Pamela had brought over a CD of the Charleston, and I put it on my portable player and set it out in the hall. As soon as the music began, tin-sounding and honky, we danced into the living room, our arms around one another's shoulders, kicking our legs out like dancers at the Moulin Rouge and then we each cut loose and did our own version of the Charleston.

Lester lowered his apple and grinned. "You girls dancing or swimming?" he asked, but he not only laughed, he clapped.

Dad got up from the dining room table, where he

was going over mail orders from the Melody Inn, and stood in the doorway smiling at us. "Your mother certainly would have enjoyed this, Al," he said wistfully. "Let me get my camera."

I was delighted that we were making a hit with Dad and Lester. If they liked us, the guys at the party surely would.

Dad drove us over to Penny's. Her house was about the same as ours – old and big, with lots of trees around it.

Both her parents were on hand to meet us at the door, and Penny herself was dressed as a pirate – short black shorts, a red shirt and black sash, gold earrings, a red bandanna, and a patch over one eye. Adorable, was the only way to describe her, but then I felt adorable, too, so it didn't bother me as much as it might have.

Not everyone was there, but most of our crowd was. She hadn't invited Lori and Leslie, I noticed, or Sam and Jennifer, and she didn't even know Donald Sheavers, but Gwen and Legs had come, and the usual gang that hangs around Mark Stedmeister's pool in the summers. I guessed Penny would be a part of it now.

The guys all came as gangsters, every one of them. Well, all but Legs. He and Gwen came as cookies. Karen was a bag of crisps, and Jill was a French maid. We made quite a picture. In fact, flashbulbs kept going off all evening, and Penny's folks took a number of group pictures.

Of course, everyone made us put on the Charleston

CD and dance, and soon the whole gang was hoofing it up. The gangsters and the flappers together looked great, and I was having more fun than I'd had at my own party.

Patrick swung me around, tipped me back, and kissed me in front of everyone; it was just a glorious Halloween. Penny's dad drove some of the kids home afterwards, Pamela's Dad drove a bunch, too, and Lester came to pick up Elizabeth, Patrick and me. Patrick kissed me again before he got out of the car.

"All that worry for nothing," Elizabeth said to me after Patrick got out. "He's still crazy for you, Alice."

"I guess so," I said. "How about you and Justin?"

"Oh, he likes all the girls," she said.

I couldn't help but wonder about Elizabeth as I dressed for bed. Justin is one of the best-looking guys in year ten. Nice, too, and nuts – or *was* nuts – about Elizabeth. But just because he made a remark last summer – a joking remark – about her getting chubby, she's been giving him the cold shoulder. It's almost as though she looks for reasons not to get too close to a boy. And she sure isn't chubby now. There are times I feel there will always be a part of Elizabeth I'll never know. I wonder if anyone feels that way about me.

I slept late the next morning and had a ton of homework, so I didn't go running. Pamela, Elizabeth, and I had started running every morning during the summer to tone up before we started term, and I'd vowed to keep it up after school began. I enjoyed running even when Pamela and Elizabeth weren't with me. Sort of my own special time to think things over and plan my day.

But now I realised I'd let too much slip by while I was getting ready for Halloween, and began to panic that even if I stayed up all night I wouldn't be able to do it all. When I looked at the course outline for English, I discovered that a huge project I had thought was due November 10 was due November 3, a week sooner.

"Don't anyone talk to me!" I bellowed, pushing Dad's stuff to one side of the dining room table and taking over the rest of the space for myself.

"A pleasure," said Lester. "Who rattled your cage?"

"Year ten is too much work!" I cried in despair. "Every teacher thinks his is the only subject there is – that you've got all the time in the world just to work on his homework. Never mind what anyone else gives you."

"And you haven't even started college, much less a post-grad course," said Lester, which didn't make me feel any better.

I had only done two problems in algebra when the phone rang.

"Al, it's Patrick," Dad called. "Should I say you'll call him back?"

"No, I'll take it," I mumbled. As I walked to the phone in the hall I wondered if I should ask him to come over and help me with the algebra, but I couldn't very well let him help and then tell him to go home. If he came, he'd want to stay a while, and I'd lose an hour or two I just couldn't afford. "Hi," I said.

"Hi. How are the legs this morning?"

"Wobbly." I laughed. "It was a fun party, though."

"Sure was," he said. "Hey, today's the last day for that sci-fi movie at the Cinema. Want to go?"

Patrick is so smart, he can do his homework in half the time, even with his accelerated programme. It's maddening. "Oh, Patrick, I can't!" I wailed. "I'm too far behind. Heart attack city! Can't we rent the video after it comes out?"

"I want to see it on the big screen, Dolby sound and everything," he said. "It's supposed to be really good. Karen and Brian and Penny and a bunch of us are going."

I was silent.

"Alice?" he said.

Maybe I should just go, I thought. Maybe I should forget the homework for once and go, be spontaneous, but I knew I couldn't. I should have planned better. I should have checked my homework due dates. "I can't," I said flatly. "Have a good time."

"Sure?" he said.

"I'm positive. I've got a billion assignments, Patrick. I'd like to, but I can't."

"Okay," he said. "Talk to you later." And I heard him hang up.

I tried not to think about Patrick at the movies with Penny. There would always be a Penny. No matter what happened in life, there would always be a girl or a woman who was pretty and fun and popular and clever, and I had to get used to it. Patrick and I were an "item," so why did I worry about it so much?

I was relieved that I actually got through the first section of the algebra homework by myself. The remaining problems were so hard and my patience so thin that I put them off until later to ask Lester. Then I read a chapter in history and started the essay questions at the end.

Elizabeth called to see if I had gone to the movies with Patrick. She'd stayed home to do her English homework, too. I told her that I was uneasy about Penny being there with Patrick.

"It's broad daylight!" she said. "You never have to worry about a guy and a girl going anywhere in the afternoon, even the movies. That's so uncool, it doesn't even count."

I felt better, and made myself a peanut butter sandwich with bacon bits. After I was finished with history, around five o'clock, I ate an apple and painted my nails, and then I started the paper for English. I figured Patrick would call later and tell me about the movie, what I'd missed and what everybody did after. But the phone didn't ring. Just before I went to bed I checked my E-mail. No messages at all.

Patrick wasn't on the bus the next morning. Sometimes he has band practice before school, and his dad drives him over. Penny was there, though, talking about the movie and how scary it was.

Brian guffawed loudly and interrupted. "There was this part where the woman's in the cave, afraid to come out because the creature with all the tentacles is around somewhere, but she doesn't know it's been cloned, and there's another one back in the cave, and you see this tentacle sort of oozing, sliding across the rocks behind her . . ."

"And then Patrick puts his hands around Penny's neck!" laughed Mark.

"You should have heard her scream!" Brian said.

"Everyone in the cinema turned and stared at me!" Penny went on, laughing at herself "He was horrible!"

"A hundred-decibel scream," said Justin.

"Well, he *scared* me!" Penny said, laughing some more.

I slid onto the seat beside Pamela.

"I think you should have come," she whispered tentatively.

"*You* went?"

"Sure. I thought everyone was coming."

"I had tons and tons of work to do."

She just shrugged. "When the cat's away, the mice will play," she said.

"What's *that* supposed to mean?"

"Just that Patrick was fooling around. He was sitting right beside Penny."

"Well, he had to sit somewhere."

"I know. I'm just telling you."

I felt I was swimming against the tide. I felt as though a big steamroller was coming at me, or an avalanche or something.

"So . . . what else happened?" I asked.

"Nothing. That I know of"

"Meaning . . .?"

"I don't know, Alice. I can't watch them every minute."

"Well, I can't, either," I said. "And what's more, I shouldn't have to."

"Right," said Pamela.

I felt flat all day. Irritated. Anxious. But I made up my mind that I wasn't going to ask Patrick about it. I wasn't going to nag and question and put him through the third degree. If you had to do all that to keep a guy, what good was it?

He called that evening. He told me all about the movie, but he didn't mention Penny. Didn't say how he'd slipped his hands around her neck at the critical moment, made her scream. How he happened to be sitting right beside her.

I was proud of myself that I didn't ask. "I'm sorry I missed it," I said.

"Yeah, it was great," he said. "You want to stop by the band room after school tomorrow? Levinson's going to decide between me and another guy as to who gets to do the drum solo at the winter concert. We both have to audition, and I figure it wouldn't hurt to have my friends there."

"What time?"

"Three."

"Oh, Patrick! I've got an editorial meeting for the school newspaper! We get our assignments for the next month. Dam!"

"You can't skip?"

"If I do, I'll get stuck with the assignment nobody

else wants. I've heard it's really, really important to be at the first meeting of every month."

"Well, that's the way the ball bounces," Patrick said.

"Look. I'll see if I can't get my assignment first and come right down to the band room," I told him.

"Okay. See you," he said.

I loved being one of the two year ten roving reporters, and looked forward to the weekly meetings. Sam Mayer was only in year ten, too, but he'd moved right up to photographer. He was so good that he was sent to cover the first football game. The roving reporters got the fluff assignments, we call them, the kind you could either put in or leave out and it wouldn't make much difference. But some assignments were better than others, and they were fun.

Nick O'Connell, in year thirteen, was editor in chief, and when I got to the meeting, there was a big argument in progress. Sara, the features editor, was complaining that none of her ideas were taken seriously, and that it was obvious to her that guys ran the newspaper, and girls didn't get much say about the way it was done. In spite of myself, I was about five minutes late coming in, and wasn't sure what the issue was. But Sara was so upset that her chin quivered, and I knew it sure wasn't the time to ask if I could choose my assignment and leave.

Some of the kids were taking Nick's side and some were taking Sara's, and then somebody brought up an issue that seemed totally unrelated to the problem, and everyone went off on that. By the time Nick got to the assignments, he started with year thirteen instead of year ten, and finally – the very last – I got mine: I didn't even get a choice. Something about the "mystery meat" served in the school canteen.

Nick said it was okay for me to go then, so I grabbed my coat and book bag and ran down two flights of stairs, then the long corridor to the band room. But everyone had gone. The caretaker was sweeping up. I took a city bus home and tried calling Patrick, but no one answered. When I called again around ten, his mum said he'd gone to bed.

Lester had to drive me to school early the next morning because I'd forgotten to pick up the new layout instructions for the school paper. At noon, they served the mystery meat again, and luckily I had my camera ready. There it was, the grey-looking burger swimming in a pool of greasy-looking gravy. I was careful not to take pictures of my friends – the newspaper frowns on cliques taking over the paper, the same kids getting their pictures in again and again. So I spent my lunch period walking around the canteen, going up to kids I didn't know and asking them what they thought they were eating, then photographed them taking a bite.

"Soy delight," said one girl.

"Squid," said another.

"Roadkill," said a guy.

"Skunk au jus."

"I don't want to think about it," said the last girl,

and I hoped I got the face she made when she took a bite.

I stopped at a one-hour photo shop on my way home that afternoon, and at least four of the five pictures turned out well. The fifth was a little fuzzy – I think she moved – but I wrote her up, anyway, and did a layout for the paper. It was a lot of fun writing the piece, actually. I started off quoting Lester: "There's a rumour that the food in the canteen is left over from the prison hospital . . ."

Later, I was just getting ready to take a bath when Jill called.

"What'cha doing?" she asked.

"Something really exciting: getting ready for a bath. Maybe even a pedicure. What are you doing?" I asked her.

"Just resting up. Finished my homework for social studies . . . We missed you at lunch."

"Yeah. I was doing an assignment for *The Edge*," I told her.

There was a pause. "You should have been in the band room yesterday," she said.

"Yeah? How did Patrick do? I haven't seen him all day."

"Great. He got the solo. We were cheering like mad."

"I wish I'd been there! I had a newspaper meeting. Who else came?"

"Penny."

A panic spread through me, sharper than anything I'd felt so far. "Only you and Penny?" I asked.

"Well, there were a few of us, Alice, but, like I said, you should have been there."

"What are you saying?"

"Penny went up and hugged him after Levinson said he got the solo."

"She did?"

"I mean, you could have just called it a friendly hug, but . . . well, he didn't push her away, that's for sure."

"Well, of course not. Patrick's not rude," I told her.

"But she was *there* for him, Alice! That's what I'm saying. She was there at the movie the other day, too, and you weren't."

"Well, that's just great! I happened to have a ton of homework then, and it was important I be at that meeting today. There have been plenty of times I've wanted to do things with Patrick and *he's* been busy. That's life. We just have to make time for each other when we can."

"I understand! I understand! I'm just telling you as a friend, that's all. But things do happen, and I didn't want you to be the last to know."

"Well, thanks, but it's just something Patrick and I have to work out ourselves," I said.

"I guess I shouldn't have bothered," Jill said, and hung up.

Oh, boy. I slid down the wall and sat hugging my knees. I imagined Patrick auditioning for the solo, looking around to see which of his friends had shown up. I imagined Penny hugging him afterwards. Patrick not pushing her away. Patrick hugging back. Patrick looking down at her and smiling.

And I wondered if, in the long run, it would have made any difference if I'd been there or not. If I'd been at the movie and the audition both. And for the first time, I sensed Patrick slipping away from me, and felt sick.

8

Heart-to-Heart

I probably sat on the floor without moving for twenty minutes, and then I picked up the phone and called Patrick.

"Oh, hi, Alice." Mrs Long said. "Just a minute. He's practising."

I could hear Patrick's drums going in the background, booming up from the basement. I remembered with a pang the drum lesson he'd given me down there once, the way he'd touched me, the tingle I'd felt, the way I'd wanted him to touch me again. I swallowed.

The drumming stopped. I heard Patrick's footsteps on the stairs, the fumble of the phone in his hands. "Hello?"

"Hi, Patrick. I've been hearing good things about you," I said.

"Yeah, I got the solo part. I get about four minutes to improvise."

"That's wonderful! I really wanted to be there, but there was some big crisis at the meeting and I was the last one to get my assignment. I ran all the way down to the band room afterwards, but everyone was gone. Why didn't you call me?"

"Well, I've been really busy."

I swallowed. "Yeah. Me, too. I wondered if you wanted to come over some night. Just hang out."

"Tomorrow, maybe. We leave for a band competition Friday afternoon."

"I know. Tomorrow's fine."

We talked about this and that for another twenty minutes. Neither of us mentioned Penny. Maybe when you like a really popular guy you have to get used to groupies – to other girls liking him, too. Maybe it goes with the territory.

Patrick was on the bus the next morning, joking around with the guys in back like always, and Penny and Jill were sitting together when Elizabeth and I got on. Jill looked the other way when I said, "Hi." Penny said, "Hi," and went on talking to Karen, who was hanging over the back of the seat. Pamela and Brian and Mark were all squeezed together in one of the seats. She kept trying to wedge in between them, but they made her sit on their laps.

Elizabeth and I slid in a seat together behind some guys from year thirteen who were arguing about a movie review.

"What's with you and Jill?" Elizabeth whispered.

"You noticed."

"Yes. She was, like, ignoring you."

"I don't know. I guess you'd have to ask her," I said.

*

I was miserable all day, and somehow the thought of seeing Patrick that night didn't help. I didn't feel as though he was mine any more, and even though I knew he didn't *belong* to me – he wasn't a possession – I just didn't feel special any longer. The Snow Ball – the first dance of the year – was coming up in the middle of December, and I wanted to feel that we were that same special couple we used to be, comfortable in knowing we'd be going to it together.

I put on my best jeans and a rust-coloured sweater that night, the gold locket that used to belong to my mum, with a little lock of her hair in it, and tiny gold earrings.

"Hello," Patrick said at the door, and smiled down at me.

I reached up and kissed him lightly on the lips. "Want to come in?"

"The leaves are blowing around like mad, and it's actually warm out. Let's walk," he said. "Have a leaf fight or something. Go get some ice-cream."

I laughed and stepped out on the porch to check the temperature. It was warm for November. I put on a white windcheater and we went down the steps.

"Didn't you ever do that when you were little? Have a leaf fight?" he asked.

"I think I just jumped around in them. No natural aggression," I said.

"We used to try to stuff them down girls' necks."

"Typical," I said. "Always trying to get in a girl's shirt."

He laughed.

We walked out in the street in the gutter where the leaves had piled up, enjoying the crunching sound underfoot. I let him do the talking – the homework he had to do for physics, his mum's birthday, the car his dad was going to buy, the sci-fi movie I'd missed, what a blast it had been . . . He still, though, didn't mention Penny, and it began to annoy me that he wouldn't talk about her, almost as though he had something to hide.

"I hear you had quite a cheering section at your audition," I said finally, as lightly and casually as I could muster.

He didn't say anything for a moment. Then, "Yeah, some of the kids showed. I usually block everyone out when I'm playing, though."

"And afterwards?"

"What?"

"Well, I heard you had quite a hug."

He smiled faintly. "Penny's real affectionate," he said. "It's just the way she is."

"I guess so," I said, hating the flat sound my voice took on. "You must have enjoyed it, though."

"Why not? I did what any normal guy would do – hugged her back. Something wrong with that?" Now *his* voice had an edge to it. I didn't trust myself to respond, and then he added, sort of jokingly, "She *likes* me! What can I do?"

"What else?" I said.

Patrick wasn't smiling any more. "Is this what tonight's about? You wanted to lecture me about Penny?"

"What I really wanted was just an evening together – we haven't seen much of each other since school started. But if there's something I should know . . ."

"Why do I get the feeling that every time I'm within six feet of Penny I have to report back to you?" Patrick said.

"I don't know. Conscience, maybe?"

"What's that supposed to mean?"

I noticed that instead of taking the usual route to the lower school where we often sat on the swings and hand-walked the horizontal bars, we had turned at the next corner as though we were circling the block. As though my feet refused to go in a straight line that would, if we had passed the school and gone three streets further, taken us to the ice-cream parlour where Penny may or may not have been working that night. I even wondered if that's why Patrick had mentioned getting ice-cream, just so he could see her.

"I mean that I keep hearing things from other people about you and Penny, but I never hear about them from you. And if she's just a casual friend, why wouldn't you mention her along with everyone else? What's so secret if she's just another face in the crowd?"

Patrick looked straight ahead. "She's not just another 'face.' She's a good friend. She's fun to be with. I expect to have a lot of good friends, male and female, through school and college, and you should, too. The more the better."

We walked a while without speaking. The truth of what he said only cut a little deeper. So did the fact that we seemed to be heading right back to my house, because we turned again at the next corner. As though the relationship, as well as our feet, wasn't going anywhere.

"So why did I have to find out about that false 'kiss' between you and Penny from a photo on our piano? Why did I have to hear from someone else about you sitting beside her at the movie and making her scream? Why did Jill tell me about the way Penny went up and hugged you after your audition, but I didn't hear it from you?"

"Because Jill's a gossip, that's why."

"But you wouldn't have told me yourself? Once again, Alice is the last to know."

"What's to tell? She likes me, I like her. She's not you, she's just different."

Somehow, the way he said it, cut deepest of all. The last time Patrick had said, *She's not you, Alice,* it had made me feel special, as though Penny could never hold the place in his heart that was reserved for me. But now I heard something else: that Penny was different, and he liked that difference. That there were qualities he found in Penny that he didn't find in me. And while that was only natural and made common sense, it hurt like anything. What it meant to me was that Patrick found Penny fun and cute and full of life, and it made me feel large and unattractive and dull in comparison.

"What I'm hearing, Patrick, is that Penny's pretty special to you," I said, but my words came out all breathy.

He glanced over to see, I suppose, if I was going to cry. "But you are, too," he said in answer.

I imagined Patrick kissing Penny the way he had kissed me; touching her the way he had touched me. "How can we *both* be special?" I asked angrily.

He shrugged. "You just are. You and I have been going out for two years."

"Just tell me this: Are we still a couple or not?" I asked, refusing to look at him, my feet plodding on ahead.

Patrick didn't answer for a moment. Then, "If you mean will we still go out, sure. If you mean I can't go out with Penny sometimes, then . . ." He didn't finish.

My whole body felt like feet. I could feel each one hitting the pavement. The more I imagined Patrick and Penny together – petite Penny – the bigger my feet seemed to be. My legs, my hands, my head felt huge, and the more unattractive I felt, the angrier I got. I didn't want to be walking along beside this red-haired guy who didn't want me any more. Not the way he used to.

When we turned again onto my street, I could see our porch six doors down. I didn't even want to walk past those six houses to get there. I wished I was there already, safe inside.

"Well, maybe if Penny's so special to you, you should just become a couple," I snapped.

Patrick stopped walking and stood absolutely still on the pavement, his hands in the pockets of his jacket. I'd never seen his face like it looked then. Reserved. Distant. "Are you asking me to choose?" he said.

"Yes," I told him. "Maybe you should just take her to the Snow Ball."

"Then, maybe I will," he said. And he turned and walked slowly off in the other direction.

I caught my breath, wanting to call after him, but I didn't. I could feel my heart racing, my tongue dry, the blood throbbing in my temples. I turned and walked as fast as I could back home, my eyes starting to close against the tears, my chin wobbling, and then I was running up the steps, crossing the porch, streaking up the stairs to my room, and collapsing on the rug beside my bed.

I don't know how long I cried. My room was full of Patrick – pictures and postcards and mementos of all the things we'd done. Pamela had even returned the Milky Way wrapper from the first bar of chocolate Patrick ever gave me; I'd given it to her as my prized possession when we thought she was moving to Colorado. Most of my notice board was devoted to Patrick.

My memories were Patrick. My kisses were Patrick's. All my plans for weekends and summers had been built around him, and now there didn't seem to be anything left – any structure to pin things on. I'd had a boyfriend for so long that I didn't know what to do without one. How would I act, going everywhere by myself? Being a single in our gang? How did other girls manage this?

There was a light tap on the door. "Al?" said Dad.

I couldn't answer.

"Al?" he said again, louder "May I come in?"

"Yes." Even my voice sounded small.

The door opened, and he stood there in his Chinos and flannel shirt, looking down at me. "What happened, honey?" he said, and came over to sit on the edge of my bed.

I turned around and grabbed hold of one of his legs, burying my face in his trouser leg, and cried some more.

"Something happen between you and Patrick?"

"I think w-we b-broke up," I sobbed. "Oh, Dad!"

I felt his hand on my forehead, his fingers brushing back the wet hair that clung to my temples. "Want to tell me about it?" he asked softly.

"It's just . . . just . . . there's this girl, Penny, and she's been chasing him, and . . ." I couldn't go on. I was putting it all on Penny, I knew. I still couldn't face the fact that the feeling between her and Patrick was mutual.

Dad did it for me. "And he let himself be caught?"

I nodded vigorously and went on crying, curling up against his leg as though it were a pillow.

"Love is really hard sometimes," he said. And I was glad he said "love." I was glad he acknowledged that I loved Patrick, and didn't modify it with "puppy love" or "school infatuation" or something.

"It's worse than being sick, worse than throwing up," I told him, my nose clogged.

"I know," said Dad.

"I feel like there's nothing left. That Patrick's gone and taken a part of me with him."

"In a way, I suppose he has," said Dad.

I was doubly grateful that he didn't immediately start talking me out of my crying jag, that he accepted how I felt.

"I feel alone and ugly and scared, like I don't know what to do next. Like . . . like I don't even know how to *act* without a boyfriend. It's all so stupid, and yet . . . oh, Dad, it hurts! It really hurts."

"I know, I know," he said.

Deep inside, however, I felt maybe it wasn't over. That Patrick would go home and feel as bad about this as I did. That he'd E-mail me, maybe, or the phone would ring about ten o'clock and his voice would be soft and gentle the way it often was after we'd argued. I could even imagine him saying, Alice McKinley, may I have the honour of escorting you to the Snow Ball? and I'd sort of giggle and maybe cry, and we'd both say how dumb the argument had been. He'd tell me how he couldn't bear to lose me, and I'd say I'd been insanely jealous, and everything would be okay again.

Except that the phone didn't ring and Patrick didn't E-mail. I had a horrible night. I looked incredibly awful the next morning – my eyes were all puffy. I wanted to stay home. I wanted Dad to write an excuse, say I needed sleep, but he wouldn't.

"Al, do you really want everybody to notice that you aren't on the bus? Do you want the news of your break-up to travel around, and everyone know that you're taking it hard?"

That, I realised, would be even worse than letting them see my puffy eyes. I wrapped some ice cubes in a tea towel and sat at the kitchen table, holding the ice to my eyes, taking deep breaths to quieten my nerves.

Lester came clattering down the stairs for breakfast. I saw him pause in the doorway, staring at me, and then, out of the corner of my swollen eyes, I saw Dad shake his head at him sternly. Les came on in the kitchen without a word to me, mumbling something about how his car needed petrol and he'd just drink a little coffee and get a muffin on campus. Then he was gone.

When my face began to feel numb, I dumped the ice in the sink and went upstairs to shower. I knew I couldn't keep anything down if I tried to eat, so I skipped breakfast and concentrated on my face. I carefully put on foundation and blusher and powder, dropped Optrex in my eyes, blow-dried my hair, and dressed in a beige top and khakis. Walking beside Elizabeth to the bus stop, I kept my face turned away from her a little, and she didn't seem to notice my eyes.

She was talking about some English homework and how she'd almost forgotten to wash her gym clothes the night before, how her shorts were still damp, and when the bus came, we got on and sat together across from Pamela. I could sense Patrick's presence at the back of the bus, but I didn't hear his voice and dared not look in his direction.

Pamela and Karen were sitting together comparing nail transfers. This time the older kids on the bus were so loud that anything we said was drowned out. They were making up a new cheer for basketball games, with a lot of bawdy words in it, and of course all the kids in year ten were drinking it in.

Elizabeth in her usual way was trying to carry on a conversation with me as though she weren't subjecting her ears to their banter. "I forgot to take them out of the dryer and they'll be a wrinkled mess," she was saying. She stopped and studied me for a moment, then leaned forward and looked directly into my face. "My gosh!" she said.

I could feel tears welling up again. "It's that bad, huh?"

"What's *happened?*" she asked softly.

I didn't answer, and she looked quickly around to see if anyone else was listening. "You and Patrick?" she asked again.

I nodded.

"You and *Patrick?*" she repeated, unbelieving. And when I didn't answer, she said, "You broke *up?*"

I leaned my head on her shoulder, swallowing and swallowing, till I'd managed to control my tears. She put one hand on mine and squeezed it, and I was never so glad for a friend.

9

Pain

I didn't want anyone to pity me, though. I didn't want to feel like "poor, rejected Alice." I was pretty sure Elizabeth wouldn't tell anyone until I said she could, but it turned out that Jill asked Patrick if he was taking me to the Snow Ball, and he said, "Probably not."

That's when Jill told Karen and Karen told Pamela and Pamela cornered me outside the canteen and said, "Alice, what happened?"

"It was by mutual consent," I said.

"Was it Penny?" she asked.

"It was everything," I said, starting to move away before the bell. Before I started crying.

"I'll be over after school," Pamela called after me, and disappeared down the corridor.

How do you look cheerful when you're crying inside? How do you act interested in friends' conversations when all you can think about is what you said to Patrick and Patrick said to you and how he looked when he said it? How do you keep your mind on the blackboard and tomorrow's homework when tomorrow seems about as bleak and colourless as a tomorrow ever seemed?

It's weird, but I was almost more depressed about breaking up with Patrick than I remember being over my mum dying, I think, because I was too young to understand what dying meant. That it was final. Forever. I remember everyone else crying at the funeral, but I kept thinking, "But when she's better, she'll come back!" The break-up with Patrick seemed pretty final to me because – even if we got back together sometime, how could it ever be the same? How could I ever feel that Patrick liked – loved – me best of all?

"Alice? Up here, please," my history teacher said, tapping the pointer against a wall map. "You can't see China out of the window."

At lunchtime, I noticed Penny studying me warily from the end of the long table where we ate, but I avoided looking at her. I found myself laughing a little too readily at Mark's jokes, being flirtatious and silly with Brian, teasing Justin Collier. It was sickening. Exhausting. Pretending can wear you out, and so, about halfway through, I just stopped talking and concentrated on my chicken salad sandwich.

Patrick wasn't on the bus going home. The band had left for a competition that afternoon, and I was glad of that. Pamela got off at the stop with Elizabeth and me, and we walked the few minutes to my house. I held up pretty well until we got up in my room, and then I lay down on my bed and started crying.

Pamela sat on one side of me, Elizabeth on the

other. Pamela was stroking my hair, Elizabeth rubbing my back.

"Alice, it wasn't about 'everything,'" Pamela said. "Nothing is about 'everything.' It had to be more specific than that."

"We just . . . we had a big fight," I said. "He came over last night, and we argued and . . . and he left. I said some things . . . he said some things . . . and . . . it's over. We just . . . just grew apart, I guess."

Pamela fell back on the bed and stared up at the ceiling. "I *hate* those words! I hate 'we just grew apart.' People say that to explain things, and it doesn't explain anything at all. Mum said it when she decided to leave Dad for her personal trainer. I didn't like it, but it wasn't exactly a huge surprise because there always seemed to be a lot of friction going on between Mum and Dad. They were always fighting about something. But *you!* Alice, you and Patrick have been going out together for so long, I almost began to believe in true love."

"We're only fourteen," Elizabeth reminded her. "How can we know what true love is when most of us have never been in love at all?"

I was sobbing again. "I *did* love Patrick," I said. "I don't know if it was real love or true love, but I really cared about him. And I thought he c-cared for me. And now he's going to ask Penny to the Snow Ball."

"He's *what?*" Pamela choked, sitting up again. "Just like that? Is that how he broke it to you? Just, 'I'm taking Penny to the Snow Ball?'"

"No. I . . . I told him to."

"You what?" cried Elizabeth.

I had to go over everything Patrick and I had said to each other. Every step we took. How we started out kicking leaves in the street and walked around our whole block, and by the time we were six houses from home, we'd broken up.

"Well, here we are," Elizabeth said at last, propping one of my pillows against the headboard and leaning back. "Just two months into year ten, and all three of us are without boyfriends."

"It doesn't bother me," said Pamela. "I like playing the field. It just bothers me about Alice and Patrick, that's all. What about you and Justin?"

"I don't think I want a full-time boyfriend. That's just not in the picture right now," Elizabeth said.

Why couldn't I feel like they did – content to be unattached? Why did I feel so incomplete without Patrick liking me, calling me, kissing me, touching me, without being his special girl?

"What you have to do, Alice, is let the guys know you're available," said Pamela.

"What am I? A hooker?" I asked, blowing my nose.

"You know what I mean. Pretend you like things this way. Flirt with all of them. Act relieved it's over."

I shook my head. "Acting's no good, Pamela. I've got to be me."

"So what are you going to do? Cry in the canteen?"

"No, but I'm not going to try to get a boyfriend on the rebound."

"Good for you, Alice. That's the worst thing you

could do," said Elizabeth encouragingly. "Just be yourself."

"My ugly, clumsy, overgrown self," I said.

"That's not true, and you know it," Elizabeth said, and I thought how recently, when she wasn't eating, we were saying the same thing to her.

"If people start talking about Patrick taking Penny to the Snow Ball, I'll tell them it was your idea," said Pamela.

"No, don't say anything. Don't go around making excuses for me, please," I said. "Just let it be. Let Patrick do the explaining."

I was almost glad my friends had come over, because the more they talked about Patrick and me, the more sick of it all I became.

I felt somewhat better after they went home, and even went down to the kitchen and made a jelly with fruit cocktail for dinner.

But by the time Lester got home from the university, I was near tears again. The house seemed so quiet. *Too* quiet, because one thing I knew: Patrick wouldn't call. He was at the competition, of course, but even if he wasn't, he probably wouldn't have called. Perhaps not ever. I struggled not to cry through dinner. Dad was working at the Melody Inn till 9:00 every night that week, going over work that Janice had left behind, so Lester and I were eating alone, and my eyes looked like two pink pillows. Every so often a tear slid down my cheek and chin, landing on my lasagna. I could see Les looking at me sideways.

"Is it . . . uh . . . too indelicate to ask what's wrong?" he said finally, almost gently.

I swallowed. "Patrick and I broke up last night."

"Ouch!" said Lester. "I'm really sorry, Al. Anything in particular, or was it just time?"

"You mean that a relationship just runs its course, and when it's time – when it runs out of steam – it's over?" I asked incredulously, my lips quivering.

"No, I just meant that in year ten, with four years of school ahead of you and another three, at least, of college, you need to run through a number of relationships, and the longer you stick with one guy right now, the more you're going to have to hustle to work the others in later."

My face began to scrunch up again, and my voice became mouselike. "I don't *want* any other guys, Lester. I want P-Patrick! I never liked anyone as much as him."

"It's hard, kiddo. No doubt about it."

"He likes another girl. Penny. She's cute and fun and petite, and I feel like a horse around her. I can't stand that he likes her so much."

"He told you he does? That he likes her more than you?"

"No, but he likes her. He says he likes us both, that he and I should both have a lot of friends."

"Chalk one up for Patrick."

"We argued, and I told him if he liked Penny so much, maybe he should just take her to the Snow Ball instead of me, and he said maybe he would." I started crying again. "Half the time I want to run over to his house when he gets home and bang on the door, begging him to take me back, and the rest of the time I want to bang him on the head and ask how dare he do this to me."

"That's exactly why they should lock up girls around the age of fourteen and not let them out till they're twenty-one," said Lester.

We did the dishes together, putting some food away for Dad in case he hadn't taken time to eat, and Lester said that the pain of a break-up doesn't go away all at once, but it does go away in time.

After the kitchen was clean, he went up to his room to study and I went to mine. But I couldn't concentrate. I lay on my back, staring wide-eyed at the ceiling, and every so often a tear would trickle down and land in my ear. From Lester's room I heard a song on his radio that Patrick's band played once at one of our school dances. I just didn't feel I could stand it. It used to be Dad who was the sad one in our family, with both Lester and me getting along in our love lives, and now it was Dad who was having all the luck, and Lester and me who were out in the cold. Lester and me and Mr Sorringer, the deputy head, who was in love with Miss Summers and isn't over her yet.

And suddenly it seemed as though everybody in the world except Dad was grieving for someone, and that Lester and I might be loveless the rest of our lives. Weeping pitifully, I got up in my socks and padded down the hall to Lester's room. He was propped up on his bed with text books scattered all around him.

"L-Lester," I wailed from the doorway.

He looked up, then reached over and turned the volume down on his radio. "Yeah?" he said.

"D-do you think we could be h-happy if you and I just grew old together?" I wept.

"*What?*" Lester said and turned the radio down even more.

"If we don't ever m-marry, Lester, we could always get a house together somewhere. I'd do all the cooking and you could take care of the garden and the p-plumbing, and at least we could look after each other in our old age," I sobbed.

Lester opened his mouth, then closed it again, and finally he said, "Correction: They should lock up girls when they're fourteen and not let them out till they're thirty. Whatever gave you a cock-eyed idea like that?"

"I don't want to go the rest of my life alone!" I wailed.

"So get a room-mate! Get a dog! Join the Peace Corps! Adopt some orphans! Al, there are as many ways to enjoy your life as there are people. Just because you're alone today doesn't mean you'll be alone tomorrow."

"But I want Patrick!" I cried. "If *he* doesn't want me anymore, how could anyone else?"

Lester pushed his books aside and motioned for me to come over and sit beside him. I was only too glad. I crawled up on the bed, leaning back against the pillows by the headboard, and snuggled up against him. He even put one arm around me.

"You're talking a little nutty, Al, you know? Aren't you the same person you were a couple weeks ago?" He lifted my face with his other hand as though looking me over. "I don't see any facial hair; don't see any fangs."

I just sniffled.

"Fourteen years ago," Les went on, "Patrick Long was just a squalling little blob of protoplasm in messy nappies who grew up to play the drums. He's just one of the three billion males on this planet, and – even assuming that he hates you, which I doubt – are you going to let that one sack of skin and blood and bones named Patrick make the decision about whether you are likable or not? Attractive or not? Are you going to let that one squalling blob of protoplasm just fourteen years out of nappies determine your self-esteem?"

I sniffled again. "I thought you l-liked Patrick."

"I do! But when did you let him have all this power over you? If *he* likes you, you're witty and beautiful; if he doesn't, you're dog doo. Am I right here?"

I just leaned against Lester and didn't answer, loving the closeness. He smelled of taco chips and beer. He handed me a Kleenex, and I blew my nose.

"The one thing about life, Al, is it's always changing. Bad things don't last forever. It's okay – it's normal – to feel depressed over this, but it won't last. Trust me."

"But if bad things don't last forever, if everything changes, that means good things don't last, either," I countered.

"True. People do die, after all. But most of us find some level at which we can be, if not deliriously happy most of the time – and nobody is – we can be reasonably content, with healthy spurts of excitement and joy. If you care about yourself, then the things that happen outside yourself, things you can't control, can hurt, but they can't destroy you. Philosophy 101."

I could tell from the way Lester shifted his body slightly that his arm was getting numb, but I went right on leaning against him. It was too comforting to give up. "Do you ever miss your old girlfriends?" I asked.

"Some of them."

"Crystal?"

"I think about her once in a while, and hope she's happy with Peter. I don't think it would have worked out if I'd married her."

"Eva?"

"I'm glad that's over."

"The dingbat?"

"Who?"

"Joy what's-her-name. Do you ever think about her?"

"Never. I've forgotten all about her."

"Marilyn?"

Lester withdrew his arm and rubbed his shoulder. "Yes, I think about her. But right now it's best if I stick to the books and forget the ladies for the time being. It's a difficult term."

I blew my nose again. I was beginning to feel more

like myself "Now that you're twenty-two, Les, do you think you're any smarter? I mean, can a person *feel* himself getting wiser?"

"Definitely. All I wanted at eighteen was my own car, a pretty girl to ride around in it with me, a six-pack, and a good guitar. And right now, none of the above is my first priority."

I started to grin. "Are you, by chance, wearing any of the birthday boxer shorts we gave you? Some of the girls have been asking."

Lester contemplated that for a moment, then pulled out the waistband of his jeans and peered down inside. "Yep," he said.

"Which ones? The boxers with newsprint on them? Ants in the pants? What does the well-dressed philosopher of twenty-two wear under his jeans?"

Lester grinned. "Daffy Duck," he said, and waved me out of his room.

10
Alone

The phone rang about five minutes later, and I dragged it into my room and sat down on the bed. It was Jill.

"Alice, are you okay?" she asked. I guess this meant we were friends again.

"I suppose everyone's heard by now," I said in answer.

"Patrick's a jerk," she told me. "It's one thing to flirt with Penny, but another to break up with you."

I could feel tears welling up in my eyes again. "He's just . . . just being honest."

"How can you defend him like that?"

"Well, he can't help liking somebody."

"Of course, Penny's mostly to blame," said Jill.

I didn't want to get into this, because I knew she was goading me into saying something against Penny, and everything I said would get right back to her. "Maybe nobody's to blame," I said, my voice flat. "That's just the way it is. She likes him, he likes her."

"Oh, stop being so noble," Jill said. "She's been making a play for Patrick for months, and everyone knows it. Of course, Patrick could have ignored her, but –"

"Listen, Jill. I've got to go. I've got homework and stuff."

"But are you sure you're all right?"

"No, but I'll live," I said.

I hung up and sat with the phone in my lap, staring at myself in the mirror on the opposite wall. I looked a mess. My eyes were puffy, my cheeks streaked with tears. I wear hardly any mascara, but the eye liner on my lower lids was smeared.

The phone rang again and I leaped, almost knocking it to the floor. I waited till the third ring, just in case it was Patrick. It was Gwen.

"How you doin', girl?" she said, in that wonderful, thick, comforting voice.

I started crying again. I couldn't *believe* it.

"Not so good, huh?" said Gwen.

"I'm pretty sad," I mewed, my chin wobbly. "I'm just . . . *really*, *really* sad."

"I know. I guess you and Patrick have been going out together for so long, we sort of looked at you as Siamese twins. Inseparable," she said.

"That's the way I felt, too," I told her. "But we're not. And now I just feel strange and lost."

"Listen, if you ever need to talk, will you call me? Doesn't matter what time, day or night, you call."

"Thanks, Gwen. But I've got Dad and Lester. I wouldn't have to call you in the middle of the night. I'll be okay."

"Sure now?"

"No, but don't worry."

I put the phone on the floor and decided to take a bath. To soak a while with a cold flannel over my eyes, and try to let my mind go blank. But as soon as I settled down in the water, the flannel slid down below one eye and I found myself staring at my knees sticking up out of the water.

They suddenly looked fat to me. Fat knees. How could I expect Patrick to like a girl with fat knees? I sucked in my breath and spread my fingers out over each kneecap. My fingers looked short and stubby, and my nails were uneven. How could Patrick like a girl with stubby fingers? It was just as Lester had said – now that Patrick didn't love me anymore, I must be unlovable. I was appealing and attractive up until I had said, Maybe you should take Penny to the Snow Ball, and by the time he had said, Maybe I will, I had metamorphosised into this ugly creature with swollen eyes and stubby fingers and fat knees.

The phone rang, and I heard Lester's footsteps out in the hall, then a tap on the bathroom door. "Hey, Al. It's Karen. You want to take it?"

"Yes, but don't look, Lester!" I yelped, spreading the flannel over my breasts and doubling my legs up.

"Blindman's bluff!" he called as he slowly opened the door and emerged with his eyes closed, feeling his way with one hand, holding the cordless phone in the other.

I reached for the phone and grabbed it just as

Lester's foot hit the side of the bath and he lost his balance, lurching forward. Both arms landed in the water up to his elbows. Water splashed all over the place.

"Lester!" I shrieked.

"What's happening?" came Karen's voice.

"Am I supposed to swim my way out, or what?" Lester asked, opening his eyes anyway.

"Don't look!" I yelped as he tried to wipe the water out of his eyes.

"Oh, my stars, she's *ne-kid!*" Lester cried, imitating Aunt Sally.

"Alice, what's going on?" came Karen's voice over the phone.

I was swinging the flannel at Lester to get him out, and he was trying to get to his feet to find a towel. When the door finally closed behind him, I said, "Hello?"

"What in the world is happening?" asked Karen.

"Lester just fell in the bath," I said. "He tripped. I'm alone now."

"Well, I just called to see if you needed to talk," she said.

"I'm about talked out, Karen. Word sure travels fast. Everyone seems to know."

"I just wanted to make absolutely sure you're all right."

"I'm okay."

"But are you sure?"

"I'm not sure about anything! I thought I was sure about Patrick, and look what happened!" My face scrunched up. "I thought we were a *couple*, Karen! A real couple. That nothing could ever h-happen to us."

"But . . . surely you've had *some* interest in other guys, Alice! I'll bet you've flirted a little with other people once in a while, haven't you? That guy from Camera Club last year who used to like you. Sam Mayer?"

"But I never gave up Patrick for him."

"Well, maybe Patrick hasn't given you up for Penny. Maybe he wants to go on liking you both."

"I couldn't stand that!" I told her. "Not after being special to him all this time. To have to share him?"

"I don't know." Karen sighed. "I just don't know. But I want to be sure you're okay."

"I'll be all right," I said, impressed that so many people cared about me. Patrick wasn't my only true friend in the world, it seemed.

By the time I got my pyjamas on and was back in my bedroom, the phone rang again. Pamela.

"All these phone calls!" I said, trying to button my pyjamas with one hand and hold the phone with the other.

"Well, Elizabeth organised a suicide watch," Pamela told me.

"*What?*"

"She's divided the evening up into fifteen minute segments and one of us has to call you every fifteen minutes. I've got the nine-fifteen detail."

"*What?*" I cried again. "Pamela, I'm okay. Really! I'm sad and disillusioned and angry and confused and jealous, but I'm not going to kill myself. Penny, maybe, or Patrick, but not myself. Joke, joke! Please don't call the police."

I put the phone back in the hallway and climbed into bed. Lester came to the door and tapped.

"Can I open my eyes now?" he quipped.

"Very funny," I said.

"What's with all the phone calls?"

"Elizabeth's organised a suicide watch," I told him.

"Come again?"

"Somebody has to call me every fifteen minutes to be sure I'm still breathing."

The phone rang again. Lester reached around behind him in the hall and grabbed it. I could hear Elizabeth's voice asking about me. "Do you think I should come over and spend the night with her?" she asked.

"Lester to Elizabeth! Lester to Elizabeth!" Les said into the phone. "There is no cause for alarm. I repeat: No cause for alarm! Temperature's normal, pulse is normal, her pupils aren't dilated or anything, and I ask you, *beg* you, to call off the suicide watch. Okay? She needs some sleep tonight. We *all* need sleep."

"If you're sure, Lester," I heard her say. "You can never tell what a depressed person might do."

"I can tell you what I might do if this bloody phone doesn't stop ringing . . .," said Lester.

"I'm sorry!" Elizabeth said. "We just wanted Alice to know we care."

"She knows! She knows! Good night!" Lester told

her, and hung up. He came back to the doorway of my room. "So *are* you okay, Al?"

"Yes. Listen, Lester, how much did you see in the bathroom?"

"See of you, you mean? I saw two knobbly knees, if you want the truth."

Knobbly knees? I had *knobbly* knees? Skinny, bony, knobbly knees? If I thought they were fat and Lester thought they were knobbly, they must be somewhere in between, which meant they were about right.

"Thank you, Lester," I said. "That was exactly what I needed to hear."

I didn't go to sleep right away, though. Dad came in late from the Melody Inn, and stopped by my room to say good night. "In bed already?" he asked. "You aren't sick, are you?"

"Sick with a broken heart," I said.

He sat down on the edge of the bed. "It's official, then?"

"I guess so."

"Want to talk about it?"

"Not really," I told him. "I'm about talked out. Penny made a play for Patrick, and he fell for it. Simple as that. I don't understand how a girl could flirt with a guy when she knows he's somebody's boyfriend."

"You've heard the saying, all's fair in love and war," Dad said.

"But *you* never . . ." I stopped, because I realised

too late what the answer was, and didn't know how to retract the question.

"As a matter-of-fact, I did. Twice, it seems."

"But you didn't know that Miss Summers had been going out with Jim Sorringer until after we'd taken her to the Messiah Sing-along, right?"

"That's right. I didn't even know her until you invited her to go with us. She seemed to enjoy our company, because when I called and invited her out a second time, she said yes. It wasn't until the third date that she explained she'd been having a serious relationship with Jim Sorringer but was having second thoughts about it. And when a man is attracted to a woman who is having second thoughts about the guy she's been dating, well . . . it means you have a chance, and there's nothing immoral about giving her a choice."

"But you said you'd done this twice. Flirted with a woman who belonged to another man."

"Well, I don't think you could say that Sylvia 'belonged' to Jim Sorringer, any more than you could say he belonged to her. They weren't officially engaged yet. As for your mother and Charlie Snow . . ."

Charlie Snow. It was a name I had heard before, and knew only what Aunt Sally had told me. That she used to think she could never forgive Dad for taking Mum away from wealthy Charlie Snow, and all because Dad wrote Mum such beautiful love letters.

"So tell me," I said.

"The truth is, your mother actually *was* engaged to Charlie when I met her. It was some party at Charlie's college, and a bunch of us guys from my college were invited. Marie was there, as Charlie's fiancée, and she danced with me just to be friendly; and we talked . . . danced and talked . . . There was something about her eyes. Like we were talking more with our eyes than we were with our lips, but we caught ourselves looking at each other the rest of the evening, and finally it was as though our eyes were doing *all* the talking."

"Sounds more like infatuation to me than love," I put in, thinking of Patrick and Penny and wondering if they'd been talking to each other with their eyes.

"I had the same thought, believe it or not," Dad went on. "And I imagine it occurred to Marie as well. You can't go hopping from one man to another, one woman to another, just because you make good eye contact."

Dad sat staring at the wall as though his thoughts were a million miles away. "I couldn't get her out of my mind, though. I saw her again at a neighbourhood theatre with some girlfriends, and we couldn't stop staring at each other. So I wrote her a funny letter, and she replied, and I wrote another, more serious, saying that I knew she was spoken for, but if she wasn't entirely sure . . . and it turned out she wasn't entirely sure about Charlie. And so she gave his ring back."

I didn't know if I wanted to hear all this or not. "If she could ditch him for you, though, she could have ditched you for someone else," I said. "It doesn't show much loyalty."

"Very true. And don't think it didn't occur to me. But she never did ditch me. Never, to my knowledge, was unfaithful. I don't know if it was because we genuinely loved each other, which we did, or whether we were just lucky, or both. You never know about love."

"How did Charlie Snow take it?"

"He was furious, of course. I would be, too. But he was also a gentleman. He and I met and had a talk. We didn't do anything stupid like fight. He suggested that we go three months without either of us seeing Marie, and let her make up her mind, but a week later there was a knock on my door, and there stood Marie. She said, 'Ben McKinley, if you don't love me, I want to know now.' I took her in my arms and never had a single regret."

It was such a beautiful love story, I felt like crying all over again. *I* wanted to be loved like that. I wanted Patrick's arms around me. I wanted his light kisses on my lips, and the way he'd rub my shoulder sometimes when I was upset. Everything about him I loved. And now, Penny would have all the things that had been meant for me.

Dad reached over and pulled me to him. I cuddled against him like I used to do when I was five.

"I miss him a lot, Dad," I said.

'I know," he told me, and kissed the top of my head.

"Do you suppose I'll ever have a love story like that?"

"You may have one even better," he said. "Life is full of surprises, sweetheart."

I pulled away finally and blew my nose. "What am I going to say when I see Patrick and Penny together at school?"

"You're going to say 'Hi.'"

We both smiled a little.

"It's going to be hard, Al, but you can do this! It's a ritual we all have to experience before we're grown – the admission price to being an adult."

"But *you* always won out! You were never the loser."

"Oh, but I was. A couple of times. There was this brunette with grey eyes, for instance, and . . . well, the spark just wasn't there for her, and she was honest enough to tell me so."

"And you lived."

"Yes. And met someone even more wonderful, your mum."

I let out my breath and looked at my father. "Okay," I said. "I *can* do this! I can get on that bus Monday and not make a fool of myself"

"That a girl! Of course you can, honey."

"But I *still* wish I could just jump from here to being married, like you and Mum, and skip all the stuff in between."

"It doesn't work that way, Al." Dad smiled. "And you'd miss out on half the fun."

11

The Hardest Part

At least I had the weekend to recover, and the only place I had to go was the Melody Inn to put in my three hours Saturday morning. It wasn't until I saw Marilyn in a new dress and haircut that I realised she was now assistant manager. Instead of straight brown hair that hung halfway down her back, it was shoulder length and curled gently under at the ends. Instead of a peasant dress or jeans and a wool sweater, she was wearing a teal-coloured jersey dress with Native American jewellery. She looked great.

"Gosh, Marilyn, you're gorgeous!" I said.

"Hope I don't look as nervous as I feel," she said. "There is so much to learn. But your dad seems to think I can do it."

"Of course you can."

"What would really help, Alice, is if you could run the Gift Shoppe on Saturday mornings by yourself. In fact, if you're willing, I'm going to ask if we can't hire you for all day on Saturdays. It would sure make things easier for me."

I stared. "Of course! I'd *love* to! Except I don't

know how to work the cash register and add tax and stuff."

"*That* I can teach you. C'mon," she said, and I had my first business lesson.

I got along fine, actually. I guess I'd watched Marilyn so much when she was working the Shoppe that I'd soaked up a lot by osmosis. Around eleven o'clock Dad came out of his office and said, "Marilyn told me she'd like to hire you full time on Saturdays, Al. What do you think?"

"*Please*, Dad! I need something to take my mind off things right now."

"All right. If you think you can spare the time."

I hesitated. "If something really big comes up once in a while, could I still get the day off?" I asked.

"We could probably arrange it," he said.

So I was hired from ten to six on Saturdays at minimum wage. I truly didn't think about Patrick again until I went back to the stockroom to eat a sandwich with Marilyn. I'd just been too busy. But we were sitting next to a brand-new five-piece Ludwig drum set that Dad hadn't put out on the floor yet, and it reminded me of Patrick. My eyes welled up, just like that.

"Alice?" Marilyn questioned. "Good grief, what's the matter?"

I pressed my fingers over my eyelids, determined I wouldn't cry, and kept swallowing until I had things under control.

"Alice?" she said again.

"Patrick and I broke up," I said finally.

"Oh, no." Marilyn sat back and looked at me, one hand dropping loosely into her lap. Then she gave me a little smile. "We're two sad sisters, aren't we?"

I dabbed at my eyes. "Do you still miss Lester?"

"All the time," she said.

"I cried so much yesterday that one of my friends posted a suicide watch," I told her.

"All needless, I hope. Alice, don't ever jump in the river over anybody. It's an insult to the sisterhood, as though he's worth everything and your life isn't worth squat. At least I'm not as sad as I used to be. I *am* getting over him. Getting Janice's old job helped. Anything that builds your self-esteem helps."

She was right about that. I worked hard all afternoon and once I'd mastered the cash register and adding sales tax and counting change, I began to think of the Gift Shoppe as my own little place. I even put a pair of men's briefs on display, with *Beethoven* on the seat, and sold three pairs by five o'clock.

As good as I felt at the shop, however, I felt awful after I got home. Saturday night, and I wasn't going out with Patrick. Of course, I wouldn't have been going out with him, anyway, because he was in a band competition at Frostburg, but at least I could have fantasised that he was thinking about me.

Both Elizabeth and Pamela called and asked if I wanted to go to a movie or something, but I knew we'd just sit around afterwards talking about Patrick and Penny, so I said that Dad and Les and I had plans.

I put on all my favourite CDs and cleaned out my chest-of-drawers. Then I sorted through all the clothes in my wardrobe and filled a couple of bags for charity.

On Sunday I studied. I even read ahead in history, had a chance to go over my algebra homework twice, memorised the new vocabulary for Spanish, and did my nails. And all the while I had a pot roast on the stove, simmering with carrots and celery and onions. The house smelled wonderful. I'll admit I checked my E-mail about six times to see if Patrick was back; if he had, perhaps, sent a message.

And around nine o'clock, I found one:

I really didn't want things to work out like this. I'd like to keep seeing you, but I need other people, too.

I E-mailed back:

We all need other people, Patrick. That's not the point. I thought we were pretty special to each other, but Penny is obviously special, too. You can't be "special" to us both.

He called. I pulled the phone into my bedroom and sat on the floor, my back stiffly against the edge of my bed; I wasn't comfortably curled up on my rug with my pillow as I usually was when Patrick called.

"You want to talk?" he asked cautiously.

"About what?" I said, which was stupid, but I couldn't think of what else to say.

"About whether you're going to get over this or not."

"Why is it *my* problem, Patrick? You can do whatever you want, and I simply have to get *over* it?"

"All I'm trying to say is that I still like you a lot, but I also like Penny. I don't know where it will lead – maybe nowhere – but I still want to go out with you."

How can a guy as smart as Patrick be so *dense?* I wondered. "In other words, you want me to be here for you so that if things fall through with Penny, I'll welcome you back with open arms."

"That's not what I said."

Now I was really steamed. "Patrick, what can you be thinking? How are either Penny or I supposed to be happy with *this* arrangement?"

"Look. None of us is tied to anyone else. You and Penny can go out with anyone you want. In fact, maybe we should just all consider ourselves friends and forget this 'special' stuff."

"Is that what you want?" I asked, my chest already cold with the sound of it.

"I don't *know* what I want right now. I still want us to go out, but I don't want to be told who I can see and who I can't. It's that simple."

"Then the answer is simple, too, Patrick. We can't be like we were if you're going out with Penny, too. How could you even *expect* us to be?"

There was a long silence. It sounded as though Patrick was toying with the telephone cord. Then his voice sounded flat and distant. "Well, I guess we'll see each other around."

"I guess so," I said. And then we hung up, and I felt like an old milk carton, sour and empty on the inside.

I woke up on Monday feeling bluer than blue. I knew that both Patrick and Penny would be on the bus, and that by now absolutely everyone would know that Patrick and I broke up. That now it was official. Patrick and Penny were free to be a couple, and even their names sounded right together: *Patrick and Penny; Penny and Patrick*. Just thinking about this hurt more than a smack across the face.

"Al," Dad called from my doorway. "You getting up? You're ten minutes late already. Better get a move on."

I forced myself out of bed and went into the bathroom to shower. What would I wear? Something Patrick loved, to make him regret we'd broken up? Something he hated, to show I didn't care? Something sexy, so other guys would pay attention to me in front of Patrick? Something drab and mousy, so nobody would look at me and I could blend into the background?

How about something *I* liked? I told myself finally, and put on a pair of black leggings, black mules, and a huge purplish sweater with a mock turtleneck collar. Also tiny purple earrings set in silver.

"You look great, Al," Dad said at the table. I doubted he really liked what I was wearing, but I thanked him for the vote of confidence.

"Sort of like a huge grape," said Lester. If you want the truth, ask my brother.

Elizabeth was waiting for me when I went outside. She didn't want me to have to climb on the bus alone. There was a slight hush when I boarded – only the older kids were talking – but among our friends – Karen and Jill and Mark and Brian – all eyes were on me. Patrick, to his credit, sat at the back of the bus with the guys again, not with Penny, but she was on her knees looking over the back of her seat, carrying on a conversation with him.

I gave a general "hi" and a smile to everyone at once and sat down by Pamela, who had saved a seat for me. Elizabeth squeezed in beside us so that I was sandwiched between my two closest friends.

"Just ignore Patrick," Jill whispered over the back of the seat. "Don't even give him the time of day."

"Why?" I said. "We're not enemies."

"Well, I wouldn't call Penny your friend exactly," said Karen, which was ridiculous, because it was Karen who had engineered that photo of Penny and Patrick and the non-kiss. Why is it so difficult to tell who your friends are and who aren't? Is this just a problem among girls? Do guys act like this? I happened to know that Penny and Karen went shopping a lot together. Whose side was she on, anyway, or did she just enjoy starting a fight?

I changed the subject and, when the bus reached the school, was one of the first to get off. I wanted in the worst way to see whether Patrick and Penny were walking together, but I went on inside and straight down the hall to my locker.

One thing I noticed was that Mark and Brian and

Justin and some of the other guys didn't know what to say to me all day. As though guys had to stick with guys and girls with girls. But I tried to stay as cheerful as I could. I said hello to the boys when I passed them in the corridor, and even got through the bus ride home again, though this time I noticed that Penny had gone to the back to sit beside Patrick.

It was the next day that it hit. I had just come out of the library and Patrick and Penny were walking about fifteen feet ahead of me, holding hands. Penny seemed to be doing all the talking, and every so often, Patrick turned and looked down at her with the same smile I remembered, the affectionate smile he used to give me, the funny little smile that wrinkled the bridge of his nose. I whirled around and went in the opposite direction, a pain in my chest and throat as though I'd swallowed a tennis ball and it was stuck.

I began to feel that every corridor at school was a minefield. I didn't want to see Patrick at all, and I especially didn't want to see him with Penny. If either of them were coming and they hadn't seen me, I'd duck in a classroom or lean over a drinking fountain – do anything possible to make myself invisible. Twice I started up a flight of stairs to hear them coming down the flight above me, and I'd turn and go the other way.

This is ridiculous! I told myself. Wasn't it enough that Patrick liked someone else? Did I have to be a prisoner in my own school, too? I knew I couldn't go on hiding like this all year, but I just didn't feel strong enough, or wise enough, to face Patrick and not see his eyes light up any more. To say hello to him in the corridor and not hear any warmth in his voice. I just didn't think I could bear it.

But after I'd seen them together, it helped to simply expect it: Patrick standing by Penny's locker, his hands on her waist, her hands on his shoulders; Patrick at a table in the library, Penny next to him, his arm around her, and the worst – Patrick and Penny standing out on the steps, kissing lightly on the lips, the way *we* used to do.

It still hurt, but at least it didn't surprise me anymore. If they did this in public, though, what did they do in private? I wondered. How far did she let him go? How far did he want to? Was it possible they went all the way? If *I* had . . .? I didn't finish the thought.

At home after school, all I wanted to do was curl up on my bed and listen to CDs. Sleep. I slept a lot. I also got my period, so I just dragged around the house and for the most part, Dad and Lester left me alone – didn't yell at me if I forgot it was my night to do the dishes, or if I left my shoes where someone could trip over them, or forgot to take the clothes out of the dryer.

I was glad I didn't have any classes with Patrick this term. I'd been so disappointed in September when I'd found out I didn't, but now I was relieved. On Thursday, though, third lesson, I went in the library to take out a book, and Patrick was there at the desk, waiting, too. We were both embarrassed.

"Hi," he said. He was wearing a white sweatshirt, and a lock of his flaming orange-red hair hung carelessly down over one eye.

"Hi," I answered.

We both glanced in opposite directions. There wasn't anyone at the desk.

"Nobody here?" I said finally.

"She's looking for a book I reserved. Said she'd be right back," Patrick told me.

"Oh," I said.

More silence. The librarian appeared, stared for a moment at the book in her hand, then must have realised it wasn't the right one and went back in her office. Patrick shifted his weight to the other foot.

I felt I would rather have a tooth filled than stand here like this beside Patrick. Have a tooth filled without anaesthetic, in fact. About the only thing worse would be if Penny came in, too, and they stood beside me, kissing. I wondered idly how Patrick would react if I reached out and touched him. Moved over and kissed him lightly on the cheek? *That cheek belongs to me!* I found myself thinking. After being my boyfriend for two years, would he push me away? Was there any of the old feeling left for me at all?

Finally I said, "How was the band competition last weekend?"

Patrick looked surprised. Startled, even. "Okay, I guess. We came in second in overall performance. We could have played better, though."

"Second sounds pretty good to me," I said.

The librarian returned with Patrick's book, stamped it, and he was done.

"See you," he said.

"Bye," I said.

I knew I'd done well. I knew things would be a little easier now that I had proved I wouldn't hold a grudge – that we could speak civilly to each other. But no-one could possibly know how much it had hurt to stand there talking like strangers when once we would have leaned against each other, Patrick caressing my arms as we waited. When we used to French-kiss, he would run his hands up and down my sides, and my breasts tingled. Where did those feelings go when you had once been so special to each other? How could they just evaporate as though you'd never had them at all? They didn't. They stayed, and stayed, and stayed.

"Al, phone!" Dad called that evening.

"Hello," I said, thinking that *maybe* it was Patrick. Maybe my speaking to him had broken the ice, and he'd changed his mind about Penny. But it wasn't. It was Mrs Price.

"Alice, I hope I'm not interrupting your studying or anything," she said, "but could we talk for a minute? Elizabeth's gone over to the library, so this is a good time for me."

I hate it when someone's parent does that – talks to me behind her back and tries to make me the go-between.

"It's okay," I said. What else could I do?

"I just don't know what's going on with her lately. With us, I should say, because she's irritable with her father, too. It's as though she's *looking* for ways to disagree with us. All we have to do is suggest something and she's against it. I didn't care so much when she gave up gymnastics and ballet, because they put too much emphasis on staying slim, and we all know the kind of trouble Elizabeth has had with that. But *piano?* Has she . . . well . . . said anything to you about that, Alice? I mean, anything that might help me understand?"

"Not really," I said. "What's happened?"

"She dropped piano. After all the work I went through to get Charles Hedges to take her on, and all the interest he's shown in her – he insists she's talented – she quit. She didn't even tell me." Mrs Price's voice trembled. "He called and said it was a shame she didn't stay with it, because she'd make a really good pianist."

"Elizabeth could be good at almost anything," I said.

Mrs Price sounded on the verge of tears. "I know. I just thought . . . if you could ask her about it. I mean, if I just *knew* why she's so uncooperative, lately . . ."

"I sort of hate to go behind her back," I said.

"And I hate to ask it, but I'm . . . I'm just so *puzzled!*" she said, and sniffled. "It's as though she has a grudge against us or something."

"If I find out anything, I'll let you know," I said, but I didn't promise to pry.

"I appreciate it, Alice. You're the only one of her friends I felt I could ask. All I want is for things to be like they used to be between Elizabeth and me – between her and her dad, too. And I think she's making a horrible mistake giving up piano."

After I hung up, I knew I didn't want to get involved in this. When a parent says she wants things to be the way they used to be, what she is saying is that she doesn't want you to grow up, because that's what it's all about. Change. Elizabeth's been the perfect daughter for so long, she can't stand it, but her mum just doesn't see that.

There must have been a blow-up over at Elizabeth's shortly after her mum talked to me, because Elizabeth was steamed all the way to the bus stop the next morning.

"I just get so tired of parents thinking they know what's best for you when they don't know what's best at all!" she raged. "All I hear is 'Mr Hedges this' and 'Mr Hedges that' . . . like he's some sort of god, and we're supposed to worship him just because he says I have talent."

"Maybe you really do," I said.

"That's not the *point!* I don't want to be a professional pianist. I can play well enough to suit me, and I don't care whether I ever get better than this or not. This year's a lot harder than last, and I've loads more work to do."

"Did you explain that to your folks?"

"They don't care how I feel. All they care about is

how Mr Hedges feels. *He'll be so disappointed. He took such an interest in you. He'll think we're so ungrateful.* Who *cares* what he thinks? *I'm* their daughter!"

"I think you all need to improve your communication skills," I said, trying to make a joke of it.

"Mum puts on that hurt look, like I've let her down. And Dad just buries himself in the computer. *If she wants to throw her talent away, let her,* he says. *We gave her the best lessons money could buy, and if she doesn't care, it's her loss – all those years of practise.*"

"Maybe you could take a year's leave from piano," I suggested. "Then see how you feel – if you really miss it or not."

"They'll never give up," Elizabeth said, and I was astonished to see there were tears in her eyes. "They've got me on this guilt trip, and they have no idea what it's doing to me."

I guess they didn't. All I could figure was that this argument was about a whole lot more than piano lessons, but I didn't know what it was.

Everything seemed to depress me lately. Elizabeth and her folks, algebra, breaking up with Patrick . . . At home that evening, Dad asked if he'd got any post and I knew immediately he meant *any letters from Sylvia,* but there weren't any. Lester had put in a couple of hours at the shoe shop after his classes at Uni, and he was tired. Now that he'd broken up with Eva, he didn't seem to be having as much fun as he used to. He spent most of his time studying.

And suddenly I said to myself, *Alice, you're not the only one who's hurting here. You aren't the only one with problems. Concentrate on someone else for a change.*

It's what they say to do when you're depressed, you know. Walk in someone else's shoes for a while, and your own won't feel so tight. I wasn't too worried about Dad, because I knew his mood would improve the minute he heard from Sylvia. And he could always pick up the phone and call her in England if he wanted. But I wished I could do something for Lester. The holidays were coming up and he wasn't really dating anymore.

Of course, with Thanksgiving only a week off, what I *should* be doing, I thought, was concentrating on someone *really* needy – maybe by inviting a poor family to have Thanksgiving dinner with us, but I didn't know any poor families personally. I'd thought of inviting Pamela and her dad; they weren't poor, but they were sad, with Mrs Jones having deserted the family. But Pamela had told me that her uncle and aunt would be in town, and they were all going out for Thanksgiving dinner at a restaurant.

So on Friday after school, I looked up the number for the Salvation Army and called. I said that I wanted to invite some people who might otherwise be alone on Thanksgiving. And then, thinking of Lester, I said maybe the Salvation Army knew of some young women who were working as maids or something, or were far away from their families this Thanksgiving, and might like to share our dinner with us.

How many people could we serve? they asked. I mentally counted the number of chairs. Six in the dining room, four in the kitchen. Then I realised I would be doing the cooking, and I'd never cooked for ten people in my life.

"Uh . . . three, I guess," I told them. That would be double the size of our family.

The Salvation Army said that mostly they had whole families of eight or nine needing a place to go on Thanksgiving, but if I got in touch with an organisation called CCFO, perhaps they would know of some young women who would be glad for a refuge on Thanksgiving Day.

I liked that – a refuge. I liked thinking of our house that way. So I called the number he gave me, and was startled when a voice said, "Community Connections for Female Offenders, may I help you?"

I blinked, then swallowed and told them how the Salvation Army had given me their number, and that we had room at our table for three young women on Thanksgiving, and did they know of any ladies who didn't have anywhere to go?

The man on the phone asked if I knew anything about their organisation, and I said no. He said that their purpose was to help women offenders, now out of prison, to readjust to the community. To help them find places to live and jobs so they wouldn't return to a life of crime.

I gulped.

Then he assured me that he would not send us anyone who had been accused of a violent crime, and they would all have places to live, but that CCFO, for their part, needed assurances that we were what I claimed we were, simply a family who wanted to share our holiday, because they don't just send three young women out to anyone who asks. After they had checked on us, he would like to call my father at his place of employment, so I gave him Dad's number at the Melody Inn.

"Very good," he said. "We appreciate your call, and we'll be in touch."

At least it gave me something to take my mind off Patrick.

A letter from Sylvia had come that day, and Dad was in a good mood all evening. He always read her letters three or four times before he folded them up and put them away, and she must have said all the right things because he was still smiling when he tucked it back in the envelope.

"Dad," I said from across the room where I was slouched down in my favourite beanbag chair that he's been trying to get rid of. "I thought it would be nice if we invited some poor people to our house for Thanksgiving this year. I mean, people who ordinarily wouldn't have anyone to spend the holiday with."

Dad looked at me over the rims of his glasses. "That's a noble thought, Al. I think it's a fine idea. Do you know of a family?"

"Well, no, but I called the Salvation Army – just to see how we might go about it – and they referred me to another organisation that knows of" – I remembered what the man at the Salvation Army had said about people needing a refuge – "refugees who would appreciate Thanksgiving in someone's home, and so I called and this man is going to phone you at work. He said they always check people out first. They don't send . . . um . . . refugees out to just anyone who asks."

"Of course not. Honey, I'm real proud of you. How many did you say we would take?"

"Just three," I said quickly. "I wasn't sure how many I could cook for." The fact was, I'd never roasted a turkey in my life.

"That's great. Les and I will help, of course. It's a fine idea."

I called Elizabeth and told her what I'd done and she said it was a fine idea, too. Elizabeth goes for noble things. She said they were having her grand-parents for Thanksgiving, but she could come over that day and help me out for a couple of hours, that she wanted to do her part for the refugees, too.

"They speak English, don't they?" she asked.

"I'm sure of it," I said, and began to wish I hadn't said anything at all about refugees.

The next day at the Melody Inn, both Dad and Marilyn were with customers and I was answering the phone when a call came from CCFO.

"Dad," I said, going over to the centre of the shop where he was showing a cello to a couple. "You have a phone call."

"I'm with a customer, Al. Can't you take it?"

"They have to speak to you," I said.

"Excuse me," Dad said to the couple, and went

back to the counter. "Hello?" I waited, holding my breath. "Yes, that's correct. I'm her father, and she told me we'd be having guests. We're delighted to have them . . . Yes, that will be fine . . . Yes . . . I wonder if I could put my daughter back on the line. I'm with customers at the moment . . ." He handed the phone back to me.

The man from CCFO wanted directions to our house and asked what time the women should be there. I hadn't even thought about it. I figured it would take most of the morning to cook, though, so I said maybe two o'clock.

"Well, we do appreciate your thoughtfulness," the man said. "It means a lot to former prisoners to experience Thanksgiving in a friendly home. One of the women will be driving the other two, and their names are Shirley, Charmaine, and Ginger."

12

Expanding My Horizons

There are two ways that putting your mind on other people makes you feel better. First, it simply gives you something to do, and second, you don't feel so alone, as though fate singled you out to be more sad than anyone else you know.

As soon as I got home from the Melody Inn on Saturday – Dad always works an hour or two after closing on Saturdays – I called Aunt Sally in Chicago and asked her how to roast a turkey. I didn't want to get into who exactly we were having for dinner, so I told her we were having some refugees.

"My goodness, Alice, you are so grown up!" she said. "Your dad must be very proud of you."

"How big a turkey should we get?" I asked.

"It depends how long you want to eat left-overs."

We like left-overs at our house because, if the food was good to start with, it means nobody has to cook for as long as it lasts. I imagined us eating turkey sandwiches for a week after Thanksgiving, and I liked the idea a lot. "A long time," I said.

"Well, then, you certainly couldn't go wrong with a five or six kilogram turkey. That's around a kilo per person, but if you're serving refugees, no telling *how* much they'll eat. And it would be a really nice gesture to send each one of them home with a little package of turkey. Why, I'll bet even a seven kilo turkey wouldn't go to waste."

"Okay, but how do I roast it?" I asked.

"The important thing to remember is to remove the neck and giblets."

"What? I have to *kill* it?" I cried.

"No, no, but it will come packaged with the dismembered neck stuffed in the neck cavity, and the heart and kidneys and giblets stuffed in the cavity below," she said. If ever I had thought about being a vegetarian, I should have made a commitment right there. But Aunt Sally continued: "All you really have to do is follow the instructions on the wrapping and you shouldn't have any trouble. Rinse it well, and don't stuff it until you are just ready to pop it in the oven. You can find a recipe for stuffing on any packet mix. You need to figure on a roasting time of forty minutes per kilo of turkey. I'll be here all Thanksgiving Day if you need me."

"Thanks," I told her. And then, "Oh, one little piece of news: Patrick and I broke up."

There was silence at the other end. Then Aunt Sally said softly, "It was the pyjama party wasn't it?"

I thought back to the pyjama party. In a way she was right. That was the night Karen took a picture of the fake kiss between Penny and Patrick, which led to the definitely unfake kisses ever since.

"Sort of," I told her.

"Oh, sweetheart, how I wish you'd listened to me. All those bodies together there on the floor . . .!"

"It wasn't that, Aunt Sally. Somebody was taking pictures," I said.

"Alice, do you mean to tell me that boys and girls were all over each other and someone was taking *pictures?* Where was your *father?* Where was Lester?"

"It's not what you think," I said. "It was Patrick and the new girl, and Karen arranged it so it only *looked* like they were doing it, but actually . . ."

"What?" cried Aunt Sally.

I decided to quit before things got any worse. "Thanks for your help," I told her. "I really have to go. I'll let you know how the turkey comes out."

Another thing that helped was my job as one of the roving reporters for the school newspaper. My piece about the mystery meat in the school canteen turned out well. Everyone was laughing about it, and the result was that the canteen stopped serving it. They substituted turkey frankfurters, which tasted a lot better, and I realised I had not only entertained, I had made a difference.

"Good job, Al!" Nick O'Connell said to me at our next meeting. He wasn't so pleased with the photos I'd taken, though, so on my next assignment, he sent Sam with me. We were to ask six different students what they would give our school as a Christmas present if they could give anything they wanted.

I liked being paired with Sam Mayer. He and

Jennifer Sadler were going out together, so it wasn't as though we were a couple or anything, but Sam had liked me last year and we were still good friends.

"You always want to catch a person alone," Nick had told us. "If you ask somebody in front of his friends, he's more likely to give you a flip answer. Get him alone and he's more thoughtful. Makes better copy."

Sam and I decided to meet before school on Friday and just roam the corridors, catching kids at their lockers, or at the juice and bagel bar in the canteen. I had to ask Lester to drive me there early, and he was grumpy.

"Lester," I said, balancing my book bag on my knees, "if you were in a position to give the university a Christmas present – anything you wanted – what would it be?"

"Al, it's seven forty-five, and I haven't had breakfast," he grumbled.

"Really, though," I said.

Lester slowed to a stop at the light. When it turned green he said, "A bike path to the university from every neighbourhood in the metropolitan area, and a babe on every bike."

"What you need is female companionship," I told him.

"I don't even have time to clip my nails, and you want me to have a girlfriend," Les said.

I was on the verge of telling him about Shirley, Charmaine, and Ginger, but decided I'd better hold off. "I know you're taking extra courses this term and don't have time for a serious relationship, but that doesn't mean you can't at least have some casual women friends," I said.

"Yeah, sure. So round me up some casual women friends," he muttered.

I just smiled and went on swinging my foot.

Sam and I met outside the canteen and found our first student sitting at a table, eating a bagel with cream cheese. We didn't want to embarrass him while his mouth was full, so while Sam adjusted his camera, I filled the guy in on what kind of a story we were doing for the paper and asked if he had any ideas of what would make a good present for our school.

"A swimming pool," he said. Then, after he swallowed, he added, "for skinny-dipping only."

I smiled and wrote it down while Sam took his picture, and we set out to find someone else.

"I heard about you and Patrick," Sam said.

"Yeah. About everyone in the whole school knows, I think."

"Patrick must have rocks in his head to let you go," said Sam.

"Well, it was more or less mutual," I told him, which wasn't entirely true. But it *was* partly because of something I had said, so I figured it was true enough. And then I added, "How are things with you and Jennifer?"

"Great!" he said, and I was glad that we saw a girl on ahead, standing at her locker, and zeroed in on her next, because I really didn't want to get in a discussion of Sam and Jennifer versus Patrick and me.

We had our six student comments done by the first bell, and all I had to do was condense or expand their replies to fill up half a page, with head shots. We got some interesting answers, though. The news editor had told us that two years ago they had asked the same question and got answers like, "Put belly dancers in the canteen," or "Reduce the drinking age to fifteen." This time the kids said things like, "Repair the school toilets and make sure there are doors on all the cubicles," and, "Build a student lounge so the kids would have some place to gather in bad weather before and after school."

"I had an interesting assignment for the school newspaper," I told Dad and Lester at dinner, glad that I could talk about something pleasant for a change instead of moping around over Patrick. And I told them what Sam and I had done.

"Sounds as though you're enjoying year ten, Al," Dad said.

"*I* got an interesting assignment today, too," Lester said sardonically. "I have to compare the moral systems grounded in Kant's Categorical Imperative, Benthamite utilitarianism, and Aristotle's *Nicomachean Ethics* in terms of whether they commit the naturalistic fallacy."

"I'm never going to college," I said.

Dad raised an eyebrow.

"Well, I'm never studying philosophy," I told him.

Elizabeth's family was going to eat Thanksgiving dinner in the evening, so she promised to come over that morning and stay long enough to help me cook our meal. I hadn't told her that our guests had been in prison, only that I'd called the Salvation Army for suggestions. Besides, I thought, everyone deserves a break – we all make mistakes. If nobody knew they were ex-cons but me, maybe they'd be treated more like ordinary people and could put their past behind them.

Lester and I went out to buy a turkey the Monday before Thanksgiving, and I remembered what Aunt Sally had said about sending some home with each of the refugees when they left. Why stop at seven kilos? I thought. Why not get a nine kilo turkey, and maybe Dad and Lester and I wouldn't have to cook for a month!

"Okay by me," said Lester. "You're the chef, babe."

I couldn't explain it, exactly, but there was something about doing a good job on that newspaper write-up, and now, learning to roast a turkey – to make a whole Thanksgiving dinner, in fact – that made me feel less lonely. Or maybe just not so dependent on Patrick to make me feel like a lovable, worthwhile person. Maybe this was a good time to try my own wings, to concentrate on learning new things. An Alice Time – all for myself.

Dad and Lester said they'd clean the house, since I

was doing most of the cooking. Elizabeth arrived about seven Thanksgiving morning.

At forty minutes per kilo for a nine kilo turkey, we figured it would take at least six hours to roast. If I wanted to serve at two-thirty, it had to be in the oven by eight.

We went down to the basement to get the turkey out of the freezer. It was so cold, I could hardly carry it, and it sounded like a rock when I dropped it on the table.

Elizabeth looked worried. "You know, Alice, I think you were supposed to defrost it first," she said.

I looked at the microwave. "So?" I said, pointing to the button that said *defrost*.

"I don't know . . .," said Elizabeth.

I turned the turkey around and looked at the print on the label. *Defrost in refrigerator 2 to 3, days prior to cooking*, it read, and I went weak in the knees.

"Oh, Alice!" said Elizabeth.

We took the shelf out of the microwave and tried to cram the turkey in, but it wouldn't fit. We were trying to turn it upside down when Lester came downstairs. "What the heck are you doing?" he asked, and that's when I lost it.

"Lester, it's supposed to defrost for two to three days, and the people are coming at two o'clock!" I wailed.

"Al, you blockhead!" Lester said, and that brought Dad to the kitchen.

Lester explained the problem. "What do you think?" he asked. "Chain saw or dynamite?"

The upshot was that they took the turkey outside, cut it in half lengthwise with Dad's power saw, and then we defrosted a half at a time in the microwave until it was merely icy. I didn't have to stick my hand into the neck or abdominal cavity to remove the innards because Dad had already sawed them in half.

Lester said he couldn't watch, but after we'd rinsed out the turkey, Dad stuck both halves together with duct tape so we could stuff it, and told me to remove the tape before we put it in the oven. Then he went upstairs to scrub the bathroom.

Elizabeth had been chopping the mushrooms and celery for the dressing, and I melted the butter and added the bread cubes. We looked at the turkey, its legs akimbo, and then at each other.

"It's positively obscene to have to stick your hand in there," Elizabeth said. "I am never going to have a baby."

"Relax," I told her "When you have children, they won't cut your head off first." We took turns spooning the dressing into the turkey's cavity. Then, while I held the two parts together, Elizabeth removed the duct tape, and we used wooden skewers to sew the bird up. At a quarter of nine, we brushed it with melted butter, covered it with foil, and put it in the roasting pan. It took both of us to get it in the oven, and I turned the heat up fifty degrees higher than it had said to allow for the fact that it was half frozen.

We did the pies next. Mrs Price had sent over some ready-made piecrusts, so Elizabeth and I made the three easiest pies in the world: pumpkin, pecan, and mincemeat. Even a six-year-old could make them. After that we tackled the sweet potatoes and mashed them with melted butter, cream, and orange rind.

Lester poked his head in the kitchen around eleven-thirty. "What time will the turkey be done, Al?"

"Three-thirty, if we're lucky," I told him.

"Three-thirty? What time are the people coming?"

"Two," I said.

"What am I supposed to do with them until then?"

"*Talk* to them, Lester! Be sociable! I'm cooking the dinner. Do I have to tell you how to entertain, too?"

"Do you know what country they're from?"

"From here."

"Refugees from *here?* From *what?*"

"I don't know, Lester! I don't know where they were born. I'm doing the best I can, and if you –"

"Okay, okay," Les said. "Pipe down."

When he left the kitchen, Elizabeth said, "Don't you know anything at all about these women, Alice?"

My heart began to thump. She was looking at me suspiciously. "Liz," I said. We'd started calling each other nicknames since we began year ten. "They're not . . . not exactly refugees in the ordinary sense. They're sort of . . . more like . . . well, troubled women looking for a refuge in an uncertain world."

"What?" said Elizabeth.

"The Salvation Army referred me to an organisation called CCFO, which turned out to be Community

Connections for Female Offenders, and after I found that out I couldn't very well hang up, could I? They've all been in prison."

Elizabeth let her spoon fall into the sweet potatoes. "What?"

"Shhhh. It's okay. They haven't done anything violent."

"Alice, are you out of your mind?" she gasped.

"Probably," I told her.

13

Refugees

We had this plan: As soon as the turkey was out of the oven, I'd put the pies in to bake while we were eating the rest of the meal. I'd heat the peas and carrots on, the top of the cooker, the sweet potatoes in the microwave, stick the rolls in the oven for a couple of minutes, open a can of cranberry sauce, and *voilà!* Dinner.

Elizabeth and I found my mum's best tablecloth in a drawer in one of Dad's cupboards. There were marks all along the creases, and the matching napkins had yellowed, but it looked better than a bare table. We also found a box of sterling silver candlesticks and ten little individual salt and pepper shakers to match the candle holders. Dad said they had been a wedding gift from Aunt Sally and Uncle Milt. While I checked on spoons and serving dishes, Elizabeth polished the silver, and I'd never seen our dining room look so elegant.

Elizabeth said she'd stay till the women arrived, and followed me upstairs so I could comb my hair and change my shirt. I chose a long, moss-green shirt to wear with black leggings, and had just put some mauve blusher on both cheeks and was fastening tiny gold hoop earrings when I heard Elizabeth say, "Oh . . . my . . . gosh!"

"What?" I turned around.

She was standing at the window, her hands on the sill, looking down at the street. I picked up the other earring and walked over in time to see the last of the three women coming up onto our porch. This one was dressed in a fake zebra-skin coat, five-inch heels, and was wearing enough jewellery to open a shop.

"Wait till Lester gets a load of this!" Elizabeth said wide-eyed. Then she turned to me. "Alice, do you think they were *prostitutes?*"

I didn't know what their convictions were for. All I knew was that Dad was probably expecting Albanian refugees with scarves on their heads, but at that moment the doorbell rang.

"Al?" Dad called from the kitchen. "You going to get that?"

"I've got it!" came Lester's voice. I could hear him walking rapidly across the living room towards the front door. The sound of the door opening.

There was a three-second silence so profound, it was as though Lester had lost the power of speech. And then the miracle happened. I heard my brother say, in his most gentlemanly voice, "Welcome to our home. I'm Lester. Please come in."

Elizabeth and I went downstairs together. The three women – two white, one African-American – were taking off their coats. They were probably in their late twenties or early thirties, and each smiled as she handed her wrap to Lester.

Elizabeth stuck around just long enough to hear the African-American say, "I'm Charmaine," the one in the leather jacket say, "I'm Shirley," and the one taking off her zebra-skin coat say, "I'm Ginger."

"And I'm Alice," I said. "This is my friend Elizabeth, who helped me make dinner. Only she's leaving now."

"Well, isn't that nice she could help you!" said Charmaine.

"Goodbye! Have a nice dinner!" Elizabeth said, slipping noiselessly past me, and whispered, "Good luck!" as she closed the door behind her.

Dad came out of the kitchen, and Lester introduced the women to him.

"You were so kind to invite us to dinner," Shirley said, pushing up the cuffs of her satin blouse, which she wore with designer jeans, and followed the others into the living room. "The CCFO has been wonderful to us."

"Excuse me?" said Dad.

But I chimed in with, "We're always glad to have company for dinner. Won't you sit down? Lester will see to the appetisers while I check the turkey." Then I made a beeline for the kitchen and opened the oven door. The thermometer still had a way to go before it reached the poultry mark, and I stared at it, trying to will the mercury to move. I grabbed a dish of black olives and a plate of cheese and crackers to take to the living room when Lester came around the corner.

"You're dead," he told me. "Al, who *are* those women?"

"Charmaine, Shirley, and Ginger," I gulped.

"I know that! Where did you find them?"

"I told you. I called the Salvation Army, and –"

"These are no Salvation Army bluebonnets, I'll tell you that."

". . . and they referred me to the CCFO," I added as Dad entered the kitchen.

"What is the CCFO?" Dad asked me.

"Community Connections for Female Offenders," I bleated.

"Holy Mother . . .!" Lester said prayerfully, and we're not even Catholic.

"Al," breathed Dad, "get out there and be friendly. Les, put the wine back and serve those women ginger ale if you have to drive ten miles to find some."

I took the cheese and olives to the living room and sat down across from Charmaine in her blue jersey dress. She seemed the most motherly of the lot. If you had met either Charmaine or Shirley on a bus, they wouldn't look different from anyone else, but Ginger . . . I figured if anyone had been a prostitute, it was her.

"So who all is in this family, Alice?" Shirley asked. "Just you and your dad and Lester?"

"Yes. Mum's dead," I told her, and instantly all three women stopped smiling and looked at me pityingly. "So we just wanted to . . . to have a feminine presence at the table this Thanksgiving, we miss her so," I fumbled, not knowing how to stop.

"Bless your little heart," Charmaine cooed.

Dad came back in the room then, and Ginger said they were sorry to hear about his wife. Dad looked quizically at me, then at Ginger, and said simply, "Thank you."

Lester found some ginger ale and brought it in with a bucket of ice.

"All three of us are looking for jobs right now," said Charmaine. "The CCFO got us work in a warehouse, but we'd like something better, if we can get it."

"What kind of work are you looking for?" Dad inquired.

"Something that'll pay the rent. Something in sales, maybe. You put yourself out of circulation a while, you're amazed at how much the rents have gone up," said Ginger.

"Shoot. Just blink your eyes and it's another thirty dollars a month," said Charmaine.

"Sales have their ups and downs," Lester told her. "I take some classes at the Uni and work part time selling shoes."

"*Do* you, now?" said Charmaine.

"A college boy!" said Ginger.

I went out in the kitchen again and turned the oven to 450 degrees. I decided I would get that turkey done if I had to blast it out of the oven. I fussed around, making sure everything else was ready to go, sat out in the living room for another fifteen minutes making small talk, and when I checked again, the needle had almost reached the poultry mark. I turned the oven down a little for the pies, and tried to figure out how to lift a nine kilo turkey out of a roasting pan so I could set it on the carving board.

I thought of calling to Dad or Les for help, but Dad had just made a joke and the women were all laughing, and then Lester said something funny and they laughed some more. I figured I needed Dad and Lester to keep the conversation going more than I needed them in the kitchen.

I slid out the oven rack as far as I dared. Then I picked up two heavy meat forks, jabbed one in each side of the turkey like handles, and tried to lift it straight up out of the roasting pan. The skin was stuck to the pan, however, so I tried jerking upward to free it.

The skin gave, the turkey jerked free, and then, before I knew what happened, one fork slipped out of the side, and half the huge turkey fell to the floor with a greasy *whump* and *splat*, followed a second later by the other.

I don't know which was louder – the clatter of the pan as it clanked back on the rack or my scream.

Lester was the first one to reach me, Dad at his heels, and a moment later Ginger, Shirley, and Charmaine were all peering over Dad's shoulder at the spectacle there on the floor.

The turkey looked as though it had been cut in half with a power saw because it had, its legs and skewers akimbo, stuffing strewn about the floor in clumps, the puddle of grease, like an oil slick, spreading slowly out beneath it.

I was on the verge of tears when Charmaine started to giggle. I saw Shirley elbow her, and suddenly she gave a snort disguised as a sneeze, and then Ginger burst out in a fit of laughter. A moment later Dad joined in, then Lester, and suddenly we were all standing there in the kitchen, howling like hyenas.

Charmaine leaned against the door frame, clutching her ribs as though she, too, might split in half.

"Well," said Dad at last. "The only sides we can't eat are the sides that're on the floor. Ladies, would you care to take a seat at the table while we tend to things here?"

"Not until we help clean up," said Charmaine. "Just hand me a dish cloth, Ben."

The next thing I knew, Dad had speared one half of the turkey, Les had speared the other, and they were lifting the twin carcasses onto the carving board. The three women, with towels and rags, were mopping up the floor, stopping every so often to laugh some more.

We were in fine spirits when we finally got the meal on the table. There was enough stuffing left in the turkey to salvage for dinner, and the sweet potatoes turned out well. So did the rolls and the peas and carrots, and I remembered to stick the three pies in the oven. Already we could detect the scent of mincemeat.

"Alice, you can cook me a turkey any day," said Shirley. When she smiled, she arched her eyebrows, which had been plucked into two thin half circles. "This sure beats jail food."

"Indeed it sure beats that," said Charmaine.

And then they began to talk. It was almost as though, once I had made such a horrible mess of the turkey, it was easier for them to talk about their own mistakes. And since the women knew how we'd got their names, there was no need to hold back.

As it turned out, it wasn't Ginger in the dozen or so gold bangles who had been a prostitute, it was Shirley, but she'd been in prison on a drug charge. Both Ginger and Charmaine had done shoplifting big time.

Once, when Shirley referred to her former profession, she glanced at me and hesitated, but Dad said, "You can say anything you want around here, because that's the way we learn in this house."

"It's the way we *all* ought to have learned!" said Charmaine, wiping her fingers with the rose-coloured nail polish on her napkin. "My mother didn't tell me *nothing!* Not a single thing I needed to know about myself. Everything I learned, I learned from the neighbour boys in all the wrong ways. I ever ask my mother a question about sex, why, she'd crack me across the mouth, like how I shouldn't even be *thinking* about things like that."

Ginger nodded. "I'd ask my mother questions about sex, she'd just laugh. Big joke. *You'll find out soon enough*, my aunt would say, and she and mum would laugh some more."

Shirley, though, was more quiet than the rest. Then she said, "My mother told me everything I wanted to know about sex and more besides. Said she expected twenty dollars a week from me – a boarding fee – for our two-bedroom apartment. Now how in the world is a schoolgirl supposed to get twenty dollars a week to pay for her own room? So I was taking boys up to my bedroom after school, making a whole lot more than twenty dollars, and that's when my mother said I didn't need to finish school to make that, and didn't care if I never went back, so I didn't."

This was news to Charmaine and Ginger.

"Your very own mama?" Charmaine gasped.

"If you can call her that," Shirley continued. "She used the money for her drug habit. Then I got into drugs as a way of getting through the afternoons with the boys. Nobody is ever again going to mess with my body and my mind if I can help it."

"Good for you," said Dad.

All the women were looking at me now.

"You got a good home here, mother or no mother," said Charmaine.

"The kind of mothers we had, you can do with-out," said Shirley.

But Ginger disagreed. "Every girl needs a mother," she said.

Dad smiled around the group. "Well, Alice is about to get one, because I'm engaged to be married next summer."

All the women began to exclaim at once, and I had to tell them the story of how I'd invited Miss Summers to the Messiah Sing-along and Dad didn't know about it, and Dad told about his trip to England, while Lester poured more ginger ale.

When I went out in the kitchen to rescue the pies, the edges were browning nicely. We sat around talking while the pies cooled, and then I set them out with a can of instant cream and some plates and forks, and we all helped ourselves.

Dad said he'd do the dishes. The women wanted to help, but he said absolutely not, so the rest of us moved into the living room and sat around our big coffee table, playing crazy eights and poker, and some other kind of card game we'd never heard of that the women had learned in prison.

"That's one thing they give you plenty of in prison: time," said Shirley.

"Isn't *that* the truth?" said Charmaine. "You ever think the months are flying by too fast, you just spend a year in jail and you'll swear that clock don't move at all."

Ginger, who was closest to Lester's age, kept directing coy little remarks to him, I noticed, and fluttering impossibly thick black eyelashes, but he didn't fall for it. He was gallant and funny and helpful and attentive, and I could tell that none of the women wanted to leave as afternoon turned to evening, but they realised they should go.

Dad and Lester helped them on with their coats, and I remembered what Aunt Sally had suggested, and wrapped up a packet of turkey and some rolls for each of them.

"Thank you so much," Shirley said, shaking hands all around. "It was a wonderful afternoon."

Ginger lingered over Lester's handshake. "Don't you

study too hard now, College Boy," she said. "You've got to have a little fun."

"I'll remember that," said Lester.

But it was Charmaine who hugged me as she went out the door. "Little girl," she said, "you don't know how lucky you are to have a home and a family like this."

I hugged her back. "Maybe I do," I said.

We watched them go down the street, Ginger in her five-inch heels that, according to Lester, would be considered instruments of torture back in the Dark Ages. And then, with a little toot of the horn, their old Buick turned around and headed back down the street.

I wondered if Dad and Lester were going to jump all over me once the women were gone, but Lester simply hit me on the head with the newspaper he was rolling up to restart the fire.

"Knucklehead," he told me, trying not to smile. "Salvation Army; Community Connections for Female Offenders. Who are you inviting next year, Al? The Mafia Wives Club?"

"Why didn't you *tell* us about those women, Al?" asked Dad.

"I thought maybe if you didn't know they were ex-cons, it would be easier to treat them like ordinary people," I said.

"Well, fortunately, they seemed to feel comfortable enough here to talk about their past, and let's hope it really is past," said Dad. "Actually, I think you did a fine thing, Al. Your mother used to do things like that – invite a neighbour in who had lost her husband. Take dinner to a friend going through chemotherapy – that sort of thing. I just wish you'd let me in on these schemes *before* they happen."

"You guys were really wonderful," I said. "You made them feel right at home. You were great."

"Yeah, well, don't go pressing your luck," Lester growled.

I went back to the dining room to help put things away. The women had been careful not to spill anything on Mum's linen tablecloth, but I decided to wash it, anyway, to see if I could get rid of the yellow lines. I carefully picked up the candlesticks that Elizabeth and I had polished, and then the little sets of silver salt and pepper shakers. And suddenly I froze and stared at the table. Five sets of shakers. One was missing.

I stood there, my throat too tight even to swallow, blood rushing to my head. I tried to picture where each woman had been sitting, and realised that the set of shakers by Charmaine's place were gone.

How *could* she? How could she accept our invitation to eat at our table and share our hospitality and then walk off with one of the few things I had left that had belonged to my mother? How could she hug me there at the door with those shakers stuffed in a pocket?

My eyes filled with tears. Angry tears. How could people come into our house and just *take* things? First my boyfriend. Now my mother's shakers. I didn't want to admit to Dad that I never should have invited those people here – that it had been another of my stupid ideas. But he had to know. I went back out in the kitchen.

"I think I made a . . .," I began, and then my eye fell on the sixth set of shakers, sitting on the counter where Charmaine must have placed them as she helped clear the table.

". . . a pretty good dinner after all," I said.

"The best," Dad told me.

When Aunt Sally called later to see how the dinner had gone, Dad answered and I let him tell her about it. Somehow, sitting in the other room and listening to his version – the frozen turkey, the power saw and duct tape, the CCFO and the spill on the kitchen floor – made me realise just how wacky the day had been, and what a funny piece it would make for the school newspaper.

When I went to school the following Monday, I talked to Sara, the features editor, about my idea, and she said sure, write it up and they'd see if they could use it. So I did. I didn't bring in the CCFO, I just said we were having guests, and titled it "The Great Turkey Disaster." Sara and Nick liked it, and even though it appeared on the last page, at least twenty kids made a point of telling me how much they enjoyed it. Maybe my "Alice Time" was more valuable than I'd realised. I was finding out I was worth a lot more than I'd thought.

14

Elizabeth's Secret

Seeing Patrick and Penny together at school was easier once I didn't feel that everyone was looking at me to see how I'd react. It was easier because I'd broken the ice with Patrick, and we always said "Hi" now when we passed in the corridors.

Part of it, I suppose, was to preserve my pride. To snub Patrick or Penny would only make me look hurt and bitter, and even though that's the way I felt a lot of the time, I didn't exactly want the whole school to know.

But I had the drama club to go to, where we read plays aloud, and staff meetings for the school paper, and the Melody Inn on Saturdays. I felt needed and appreciated, and that took some of the loneliness away.

And then, of course, there was Christmas, a plus and a minus both. I was used to thinking of Patrick at Christmas – of shopping for a gift for him, and knowing that he'd be over sometime during the holidays to bring one to me. Waiting for that extra-special Christmas kiss. And there was also New Year's Eve. Now, he was probably spending it with Penny.

But there was the house to decorate for Dad and Lester, and a gift to buy for Sylvia (Dad said we'd send them airmail express to make sure she got them in time), and presents for everyone else on my list.

"Al, the decorations look great!" Dad said on Saturday morning as I was draping tinsel, a strand at a time, over a wire strung above the shelves in the Gift Shoppe where we keep the Beethoven mugs and Scarlotti scarves and the Brahms T-shirts and the Liszt notepads (with CHOPIN LISZT printed at the top). I had arranged shiny gold and silver balls among the gift items, and the tinsel reflected the light and cast an icy, metallic shimmer over the merchandise.

"What are you giving Sylvia for Christmas?" Marilyn asked me later. She was looking pretty stunning herself in a red dress with little gold earrings in the form of a tree ornament at each ear.

I showed her the sterling silver pin I'd picked out for Sylvia from the gift wheel – the large revolving case next to the counter. You press a button, and the wheel begins to rotate. If a customer sees a ring or cuff links that interest her, she can press the button to stop the wheel, and then I open the case with a key and get it for her.

"Oh, Alice, it's just perfect for Sylvia!" Marilyn exclaimed, fingering the silver musical treble clef sign.

I was pleased that she thought so. "I decided that since it was the Messiah Sing-along that brought her and Dad together, a treble clef sign would be a reminder of that, of something they have in common," I said.

"You're going to make a very thoughtful step-daughter," Marilyn told me.

I beamed. "And she'll make the perfect stepmum."

The feature story that Sam Mayer and I had put together turned out well, though he thought his photographs should have been better. Sam is a little shorter than Patrick, and more stocky, but he's nice looking in his own way.

"They're too posed," he said. "I should have taken a few with their mouths open. Gesturing or something."

I folded up the issue of the school paper and stuck it in my notebook. "Are you always so hard on yourself?" I asked.

"You have to get used to criticism if you go into photo journalism," he said.

"That's what it's going to be for you?"

"Yeah, I've decided."

"It must be nice to be sure," I said.

As we left Room 17, where we hold our staff meetings, we almost collided with a girl carrying a huge papier-mâché icicle, covered with glitter, on her way to the gym, where they were decorating for the Snow Ball. I had *really* been trying not to think of the Snow Ball. Didn't want to remember that Patrick and I had been dating for two years, and when the year nine dance finally arrived, the one big dance we would attend, Patrick was sick and couldn't go. Now he would be dancing with Penny. She'd be wearing a glittering gown, he'd have his arms around her, and . . . "About ready for Christmas?" I asked quickly, refusing to dwell on it.

"Mum and I usually go to the movies at Christmas," Sam said.

I'd forgotten he was Jewish. "Oh. Right," I said.

"But this year I'll probably go over to Jennifer's for a while. Christmas is pretty big with her."

"Yeah. Us, too," I said.

We said goodbye at the water fountain, and I went off to my locker, deciding to invite Elizabeth and Pamela to stay over the night of the Snow Ball. Neither of them was going, either. It seemed that not too many of our year were going to be there. I guess we still all felt a little green, like we wanted to sit things out for a year and see how they were done.

Jill had been invited by a guy from the year above, though, and Brian was taking some girl from another school. But Karen was going to help serve at a holiday party her dad was giving, and Sam and Jennifer were going ice skating with Gwen and Legs, so I was glad to have Elizabeth and Pamela for company, and they were happy to have some place to go. Dad and Lester had gone to a movie, and we had the house to ourselves. I have our old twelve-inch TV in my room, so we made some caramel popcorn in the microwave and took it upstairs.

There are times you really, truly appreciate your friends, and this was one of them. I think Elizabeth and Pamela were feeling it, too. We'd been particularly close since Pamela had come back from Colorado, where she'd tried living with her mother and it hadn't worked. And whatever had been going on with Elizabeth last summer when she put herself on starvation rations only made us realise how vulnerable she was; how vulnerable we all were. Now it was my break-up with Patrick that bonded us closer still, and as I sprawled out on my bed beside Pamela, I actually felt I would rather be here with my best friends than anywhere else I could think of.

Elizabeth had heard all about our Thanksgiving with the three women from CCFO, but Pamela didn't know the details, so I filled her in. She was fascinated.

"I've never actually *seen* a prostitute," she said, reaching for a handful of popcorn and then her Coke. "Not one I was sure of, anyway. How did she act, Alice? Did she try to put the make on your dad or Les?"

"She *used* to be one, Pamela. Ginger was more flirtatious than Shirley, actually."

Pamela lay back on the bed in her black jeans and red sweater. "Can you even imagine it?" she said. "I mean, to stand on a street corner and get in a car with the first guy who stopped? Why, he could have AIDS! He could be a serial killer!"

We were quiet for a moment, wondering about it.

"Shirley said her mum got her into prostitution to help pay for her mum's drug habit – her *mum's*! And then Shirley started taking drugs just to get through the afternoons she had boys in her room," I said.

"In her pants, you mean. Imagine hating sex so much you'd have to drug yourself to do it," said Pamela.

Elizabeth was sitting over in the corner in my leopard-print chair, her knees drawn up to her chest, hugging them close to her body. "What I can't understand is how a mother could *do* that – *make* her daughter invite guys up to her room," she said. "Couldn't she even imagine how Shirley might have felt about it?"

"Ha!" said Pamela. "She probably didn't care! My mum sure doesn't care what happens to me! I could be in all kinds of trouble here, but as long as she's got Mr Wonderful in Colorado, that's all that matters."

"She does care for you, Pamela, she's just all wrapped up in herself right now," I told her.

"Thank you, Alice, for your kind words, but she's all wrapped up in her personal trainer, that's what," Pamela said bitterly.

"I'll bet most prostitutes' mothers don't know what their daughters are doing. No-one tells her mother everything, you know. I can't imagine telling Sylvia every single thing I'm doing or thinking. Not that I'd be doing *that*!" I said.

"Even when we're little, we don't tell them everything," Pamela agreed. "I remember when I was five or six, I used to go to a playground and there was a girl who threw rocks at me. She said I couldn't come there unless she said so, and for a whole summer I stayed away and never told my parents why."

I was looking through the *TV Guide* and found a movie called *Dark Secret, Hidden Life*, about a girl who had a baby without anyone knowing. It would be on in ten minutes, so we decided to watch that.

"You keep hearing about girls being pregnant and no-one knowing, but how is it possible?" I said. "Couldn't her mother tell? What about P.E.?"

We tried to imagine how a girl could keep it hidden. "Maybe she just wore baggy clothes and never did P.E.," Elizabeth said.

"But how can you keep a secret for nine whole months? Well, five, anyway, because that's when you'd really start to show if you were pregnant. How could a girl keep a secret like that from her mother for five months?" I asked.

"I can imagine keeping a secret from my mother, but I don't think I'd try to keep one from you guys," Pamela said. "When I think of all the times you've been here for me . . ."

I nodded. "We can talk about things we'd never tell anyone else. All the embarrassing stuff! Remember when you were showing us that new bra, Pamela, and Mark sneaked up behind us and grabbed it out of your hands and took it to the top of the monkey bars?"

"And the time you lost your bikini bra in the ocean?" Elizabeth told her.

"How about you learning to use tampons at the pool?" Pamela said to Elizabeth. "And your first pelvic exam." She turned to me. "And the day at school when you found out Miss Summers was going to England for a year, and we followed you into the toilets . . ."

"I don't know what we'd do without each other," I said to them both. "I hope we can still get together and talk like this when we're fifty."

"I don't think any of us could keep a pregnancy secret. We couldn't go for five *minutes* without telling someone, could we, Elizabeth?" said Pamela.

But Elizabeth didn't answer. The movie was on, and she came over to the bed where we were lying, and we all watched together. It was about a sixteen-year-old girl on trial for throwing her new-born baby in a skip. Most of it was flashbacks, about how she'd lost her father as a little girl and missed him, but her mother had her hands full trying to support them and didn't give her the love she needed, so she threw herself at the first guy who came along.

It was a made-for-TV movie, actually, but the last part was really sad, when the judge sentenced her to thirty years, and when she stared at him in the court-room, all she could see was her father. It had the three of us in tears.

"It didn't have to happen!" Elizabeth wept, blowing her nose. "If the mother had paid the slightest bit of attention, she would have seen what was going on."

"The mother had all kinds of problems herself, Liz," I said.

"Oh, I don't think the mother really cared," put in Pamela. "She was only concerned with her own pain."

"When you're a parent, it's your job to see how your kids are feeling," said Elizabeth, still choked up about the movie.

"What else could the mother have done?" I asked.

Elizabeth jerked angrily around and glared at me. "Look at the way she practically *encouraged* her daughter to go out with the guy. All she could think about was maybe he'd marry Marcie and take her off her hands. If she'd just once put her arms around her and asked how she really f-felt about the guy, and gave her a chance to ... to ..." And suddenly Elizabeth was sobbing. *Sobbing.*

I picked up the remote and muted the sound. Both Pamela and I scrambled to a sitting position and stared at Elizabeth, who had drawn up her knees and was lying there in the foetal position, crying huge, heaving sobs.

Pamela reached out and put her hand over Elizabeth's, and Elizabeth's fingers closed around it and held on as if she were drowning. All we could do was stare and keep repeating, "Liz, what *is* it? What is it?"

Elizabeth's cheeks were burning. "I ... I ... I've got to tell you something. I've kept a secret for seven *years*, and never told anyone before, not even the priest!"

This really got our attention.

"Okay," I said, wondering.

"Can you promise n-never to t-tell anyone? Especially my folks. Because if you can't" – she gulped – "I can't tell you."

Pamela promised right away, but I wasn't so sure. "I don't know, Liz. If you're thinking of doing something terrible to yourself, I'm not going to keep it secret."

She rolled over and slowly sat up, her hair tangled, her nose clogged. I gave her a tissue. "It's something that's already happened, and nobody but you can ever know about it. *Ever!*" she said.

So I promised.

But all Elizabeth did was put her hands over her face and cry some more.

"What *was* it?" Pamela asked, reaching over to rub her back.

That seemed to give her courage. "A . . . a long time ago," she said, between sobs, her chin quivering, "a man . . . a man molested me."

"What?" Pamela said.

"*Who?*" I asked. I had this awful thought that maybe it was her father and she didn't want her mother to know. But it wasn't.

Elizabeth finally stopped crying and took a minute to blow her nose. "He was a . . . a family friend. Someone my folks had known in college. A biologist, I think. Sometimes he came to our house on holidays, or when he had a conference in Washington. That's where we were living then."

Neither Pamela nor I said a word. It was such a revelation – I mean, who would have expected this from *Elizabeth!* – that we didn't know what to say

She took a deep breath and continued: "I think I was about seven, in year three, because I can remember the dress I was wearing the first time it happened. A sundress. This man's wife had either died or they'd just divorced or something, and he'd come to Washington for a meeting – he lived out of state – and came a day early to visit us. We were living near Rock Creek Park, and he always brought a little present for me – a really nice gift – a puppet or a microscope or something. My folks thought he was wonderful. I did, too, at first. He was supposed to have done a lot for ghetto kids – got them scholarships and things . . ."

Elizabeth's voice was still shaky but it was getting stronger; "Well, on this one visit, he asked if I wanted to go on a 'secret nature walk,' just he and I, and my folks said, why, wouldn't that be fun. It was hot, and we went down into the park. And he showed me lots of 'secrets' – like the bugs and worms under a rock, moss growing on a tree, a cicada carcass – the kinds of things that interest a child."

She stopped and began to blush.

"You don't have to tell us anything if you don't want to," I said.

"Shut up, Alice. I want to hear!" said Pamela.

Elizabeth went on. "We came to this big rock – boulder, really – and he led me around behind it and told me to look real hard in a crevice in the rock where there were leaves and dirt, and see if I could find anything. He had . . . he was leaning on me from behind, his arms around me, his face against mine, like he was helping me look. And he brought his hands up under my dress in front and just . . . just casually rubbed my stomach, and then he . . . slipped one hand down inside my pants and" – she swallowed "– and stroked me between my legs."

"What did you *do?*" Pamela asked.

"That's the part I can't remember," Elizabeth said guiltily. "I *think* I squirmed away, and he just laughed and let me go. And on the way back to the house he said to remember that this was a *secret* walk, wasn't it, that he and I had a lot of secrets, and we wouldn't tell anyone about them, would we, because nobody else would understand."

"The creep!" Pamela said.

"And when we got back, my parents were doing the dishes, because I can remember a big white plate in my father's hands, and it looked like a big white eye staring at me. Mother asked what all we had seen and the man winked at me and said, oh, we couldn't tell, could we, but we'd seen all sorts of wonderful things. I just nodded yes. I really thought . . . for a long time I thought this . . . that my parents knew what he was going to do and had let me go because he was such a good friend."

"And he did it again?" I asked.

"I think there was just one other time. Maybe two, I'm not sure. But the time I remember, he brought me a little box full of drawers, and each drawer had a tiny carved wooden animal in it. It was a great present; I really loved it. He called it the 'secrets' chest. And when he asked if I wanted to go on another secret walk, I said okay, because my parents were smiling at me and I knew they expected me to go.

"He said we'd need a sieve, and Mum gave me one. This time I had on shorts and a T-shirt. And we went down in the park again, and this time we walked right along the rocks in the creek, and we tried to see what I could catch in the sieve – little water bugs and things. And then when we started home, he led me through some bushes and he was talking about how lonely he was, because his wife wasn't with him anymore, and he wondered if I would do something for him . . ."

Pamela let out her breath. We waited.

"And he . . . he asked me to stand very still and let him touch me. I let him lift me up to stand on a rock or something, and he pressed against me from behind and put his fingers down my pants again, and then we went home and he thanked me for helping him not to feel so lonely anymore."

"And your parents still didn't catch on?"

Elizabeth's face was all scrunched up again. "I still thought maybe they *knew!* That they wanted me to do this for him. He was one of their best friends, and I felt I should do whatever he said. It was only a couple years ago, in thinking about this, that I began to see they simply thought it was a game. It was all in fun, our walks. But *I* took their smiles to mean they knew what he was doing to me. How could I have been so dumb?"

"Elizabeth, you were only seven!" I said.

"Eight, by then. And when I got home that day and went to the bathroom, I found that my shorts and shirt were wet and sticky at the back and I changed them, and rinsed them out under the tap. When Mum asked why I'd changed my clothes, I told her I'd just got wet, and I guess she figured I'd slipped in the creek or something."

"It must have made perfect sense to them," Pamela said. "The walk to the creek . . . the . . . the biologist . . . the trusted friend. Who would have thought?"

Elizabeth pressed the palms of her hands hard against her cheeks, sliding them up over her temples as though wanting to wipe the skin right off her forehead. "The thing is . . . the thing is . . . when he touched me, it . . . it felt good. I didn't think we should be doing that, but he wasn't hurting me, physically, and even later – years later – any time I thought of telling Mum about it, I couldn't, because I felt I was as guilty as he was. Because it had felt good . . . what he did."

So many things came to mind just then – the way Elizabeth had always reacted to talk about sex and bodies, the way she embarrassed so easily. All her emphasis on sin and confession – her mother never struck me as being that way particularly.

"Elizabeth," I said. "If a guy touches you without your permission and you get a ping out of it, it doesn't mean you did something wrong. When somebody touches the right button, you ping, that's all!"

She was thoughtful. "The next time he came, the next summer when I was nine, it was raining, and he didn't say anything about a secret walk. He and my folks were talking in the living room and I went down in the basement to play with this big Victorian dolls-house my dad had set up for me. After a while this man came down to see it. Dad and Mum came, too, and then the man sat down on a chair and he was sort of playing along with me, making silly things happen to the dolls. Dad and Mum stayed for a while, we were all laughing at him, and then they went upstairs and he stayed. For a while we were having fun. And then . . ."

I began to notice anger in Elizabeth's voice. "Then he said it was too bad we couldn't go for one of our walks, but did I want to *see* something secret? And he took one of my hands and . . . and put it on his trousers. I could feel his penis underneath . . . and I pulled away from him and went upstairs to my room. I remember walking very deliberately; I didn't run or anything because I didn't want my parents to know I was walking out on him. I mean . . . believe it or not . . . it seemed so rude, and I just told Mum I was going to play in my room a while."

"What'd the guy do? Follow you up there?" Pamela asked.

"No. He came up from the basement and played the piano a while, and then he and Dad and Mum sat around talking the rest of the evening. When I got up the next morning, he'd already left for the conference."

"When did you see him again?" I asked.

"I didn't. About four months later he was killed in a car accident, a really freak accident, my dad always said. And . . . and it was like . . . like I'd made it happen."

"But you didn't!"

"I know, but the fact is, I was *glad* when I heard it. Mum cried when we got the news, and Dad had tears in his eyes, but I wasn't sad at all, and they kept looking at me, like, what was wrong with me? This wonderful man who brought me presents and was respected in his field and had done so much for ghetto kids, and I wasn't even sad? And finally . . . finally . . . I made myself cry, not because I was sorry he died, but because my parents were so d-disappointed in me!"

Elizabeth broke down again, and I began to see how problems can get so complex, how all these different feelings could get mixed and matched in your head, and be so hard to get out later. I couldn't help but wonder about myself . . . feelings I might have had, or still have, about my own mother when she died.

I don't know how Pamela and I knew what to do just then, but it seemed like we did the right thing: We hugged Elizabeth, Pamela on one side of her and I on the other, so that we were sort of a warm moist ball of arms and faces, and I think that without quite knowing it, we were making Elizabeth feel safe with us and protected. We just let her cry, and she cried softly, like a little mouse, until she was limp and drained. When we let her go, she sat there on the bed with her head on her knees.

"You know, Liz, you aren't going to be really free

of this till you tell your folks," I said finally. "They really need to know."

"Why?" she asked, looking up at me, her face all streaked. "First, I'm not sure they'll believe me. They'll say I must have imagined it, or that it happened so long ago, I'm getting fact and fantasy mixed up. Or if it really happened, why didn't I tell them before? He was their best *friend*, Alice! Everyone loved him. Everyone but me."

"They need to know because they love you, and it's a part of you that's hurting," I told her.

"But I'm probably just as guilty as he was. I didn't try to stop him, except for that last time. He said *stand still* so I did. I could have pushed him away."

"You were eight years old, Elizabeth! That's year four!" I said. "And it wouldn't have made any difference if you were older, because he was the adult and you were the child. Look! We're considered minors till we're eighteen, right? Up until then, adults are supposed to know best and we're supposed to obey them, and that's exactly what you did."

"Well, I'm not telling Mum. It would just kill her. Let them remember him the way they think he was. But I feel better having told you," Elizabeth said.

We sat up another hour after that, talking. We heard Dad and Lester come in and go to bed, and when we finally turned out our light around one, Pamela and I in my double bed and Elizabeth on the cot under the window, I decided I was pretty sure what I wanted to do as a career. I truly did want to be a psychologist, someone who works with children before little problems become big ones. Someone who, maybe if she'd seen Elizabeth when she was eight or nine, could have helped her get the feelings out before they took up so much space in her life.

15

The Test

It turned out that Patrick and Penny hadn't gone to the Snow Ball, either, Jill told me. She stopped by the Melody Inn the next day to show me pictures of herself and the guy who had taken her to the dance. Jill had worn a white strapless dress, and her bosom was bulging over the top. If she'd sneezed, she would have popped right out.

I wondered what it meant that Patrick hadn't taken Penny, or whether it meant anything at all. But mostly I was thinking about Elizabeth. I couldn't get her out of my mind – what it must feel like to go five or six years hiding a secret like that and feeling guilty about it.

Nevertheless, I had work to do, and Marilyn and I spent the day restocking the display of Christmas CDs near the front of the shop and making sure we were caught up on telephone orders. We left at the usual time, but Dad said he'd work another hour or two.

When I walked in the house, I could hear Lester rummaging about the kitchen, making dinner, but there was a message for me to call Karen, so I did.

"Alice," she said as soon as I dialled her number. "I

didn't think I ought to call you at the Melody Inn. Is your dad home?"

"No. Why?"

"I just need to tell you something when he's not around, and I'm not even sure I should be telling you in the first place."

"What are you talking about?" I asked, puzzled.

"Well, I was at my dad's last night. I told you he was giving this party, and I was, like, helping out. Dad and Jim Sorringer are friends, you know. He bought that engagement ring for Miss Summers last February at Dad's jewellery store, remember? The ring she turned down? Anyway, Sorringer was there at the party, and at one point he was at the buffet table with his back to me – I was gathering up dirty glasses – and a woman asked him how he was going to spend the holidays, and I heard him say he was going to England. I . . . I just thought you should know."

At the first mention of Jim Sorringer I had felt a wave of cold rush over me, but now it felt as though I had swallowed an ice cube, and I wasn't even sure I could breathe.

"Alice . . . I . . . I didn't know if I should say anything . . ."

I tried not to sound worried. "Did he . . . say any more? Did he say he'd be going to Chester?"

"Yes. That's exactly where he said he'd be going. The woman said wouldn't Christmas in London be wonderful? and Jim said that actually he'd be spending it in Chester."

I wanted to throw up. "Well, there could be all kinds of explanations, I suppose," I managed to say. "There's no law that says he can't go to England."

"I suppose so. It probably doesn't mean anything at all. Maybe he's going with someone else and he's just stopping by to say hello to Miss Summers," Karen said quickly.

"Was he with anyone at the party?"

"No," she admitted. "He came alone."

"Well, thanks, anyway, Karen," I said.

"Yeah, thanks for nothing," she said apologetically. "I just thought you should know, that's all."

After I hung up, I wondered if I was having a heart attack. If a fourteen-year-old girl could actually expire from anger and disappointment. And suddenly I lost it. I went stumbling out to the kitchen.

"*I hate* her!" I said, breaking into tears. "She's a liar and a cheat, and I *hate* her!"

"Who was that?" Lester asked.

"Karen."

"What did she do?"

"Not Karen. Miss Summers! Mr Sorringer is going there for Christmas!"

Lester stopped chopping onions and stared at me. "When did you hear this?"

"Just now." In shaky fits and starts I told him about the party at Karen's dad's, and what Karen had heard Jim Sorringer say. "That's why she didn't want a diamond!" I wept. "That's why she didn't want any engagement ring at all! She didn't want to be wearing one when Jim came for Christmas! And she told Dad she'd be *travelling* during the holidays! Travelling with *Jim*, that's what!"

Lester put the knife down and leaned against the counter. I had expected him to say it wasn't any of our business. I expected him to say that this was between her and Dad, but this time he didn't. "How do you know Karen's telling the truth – that she isn't just stirring up trouble?" he asked.

"Well, what she told me before was true – about Jim Sorringer buying Sylvia a ring. I don't think she'd lie about this. She didn't sound as though she was trying to make trouble."

Les was thoughtful. "Well, there may not be anything to it," he said, "but this time, I think Dad ought to know. Maybe he already does. Maybe it's Sylvia's final goodbye to Jim or something – her way of making sure she's doing the right thing."

"How can you say that?" I shouted. "If she's not sure of Dad, then they shouldn't be engaged. Is she going to go on seeing Jim Sorringer for the rest of her life to make sure she did the right thing marrying Dad?"

"Well, let's not jump to conclusions. Let's tell Dad as calmly as we can and let him handle it in his own way."

But now the tears were really rolling. All my resolutions about not crying at every little thing . . . "It's two weeks before Christmas, Lester! Dad's been so happy. She'll break his heart. What I want to do is call Sylvia myself and tell her what she's doing to him."

"You'll do nothing of the kind. We're just going to tell Dad what you heard, and that's all . . ."

The front door closed, and Dad's footsteps sounded in the hall. I froze. He walked straight into the kitchen and looked at me. "Well, what's all this?" he said jovially. "Has somebody called off Christmas?"

That made it even worse, because someone *had*, I wanted to say. Sylvia Summers, that's who, but I didn't trust myself to answer, so Lester answered for me.

"Al heard a disturbing piece of news just now, Dad. Karen was helping out at her father's Christmas party last night, and Jim Sorringer was one of the guests. Karen overheard him tell a woman that he would be spending Christmas in England. In Chester, to be exact."

Dad stared at us as though Lester were speaking Norwegian, as though Les weren't making a bit of sense. He reached out, opened the fridge, took out a bottle of cranberry juice, and set it on the counter. And two seconds later, just as mechanically, he put it back in again, his eyes unblinking. "Well, he'll find Sylvia gone. She'll be travelling," he said, but his face looked blank. Then he added, "It's possible that Jim's just doing some travelling himself. A coincidence, maybe."

We all knew the answer to that. London? Possibly. But, Chester? No.

"Was he going alone, do you happen to know?" Dad asked, looking at me. "Maybe he's travelling with a friend."

"I don't know. But Karen said he came to the party alone," I told him. And then I lost it again. "Dad, I'm so sorry," I wept. "I *hate* Sylvia!"

"Now, don't say that, Al. There could be a good explanation. We didn't hear all the facts," Dad said, but he didn't convince me.

"*Call* her!" I said. "Ask her what it's all about."

"No." Dad was firm. "I'll let her tell me herself without any prodding from me." And then he added, "She's supposed to call tonight, and she'll undoubtedly explain it then. Now, what are we having for dinner?"

I couldn't bear it. I couldn't stand the hurt in his eyes, his voice, his face . . . I blindly reached for the plates and set the table.

Dinner was a sober affair. I think we all ate the burritos without tasting. It looked as though our mouths were scarcely moving, as though we weren't even chewing.

"How are things at the shop?" Lester asked finally. "Business has been nonstop at the shoe shop."

"We sold two baby grands this week," Dad said. But his voice was flat, and the conversation died after that.

I did the dishes after dinner, and Lester and I went right on up to our rooms because we knew it was close to midnight in England, and Sylvia would be calling Dad any minute now. We wanted him to have the downstairs to himself so he could talk to her in private. I spread out my homework on my bed, but left the door ajar. When the phone rang and I heard

Dad pick it up, I'll admit that I got up and went to my doorway.

"Oh, Sylvia, it's so good to hear your voice," Dad said. ". . . I know. I miss you, darling . . ." There were murmurs, words I couldn't make out. Then I heard Dad telling her about work and the big pre-Christmas sale at the Melody Inn. I changed position and waited. "How I wish you could be in my arms at Christmas," Dad was saying now. "How *will* you spend the day, sweetheart?" He was fishing, I knew. Giving her every opportunity to tell him. More silence. Then, finally, "Oh . . . uh-huh . . . I see . . . well, that might be fun . . . No, I won't try to reach you then, but you'll be calling me?"

She *wasn't* telling him! Whatever she said was a lie. I went back and sat on the edge of my bed, waiting for Dad to come up and tell us what she'd said. When we heard his footsteps on the stairs, both Les and I came to the doors of our rooms. Dad paused on the next to the top step, his hand on the banister.

"What did she say?" I asked.

"Well, she didn't mention Jim. I guess she plans to do her travelling just after Christmas, between Christmas and New Year's. I asked what she'd be doing Christmas Day, and she said that one of the teachers had invited her to have dinner with her family, and she'd be out most of the time, but she'd call me that evening."

"And you didn't ask her about Sorringer?" I wanted to know.

"No . . . Whatever her reasons, she's keeping them to herself But I trust her –"

"I can't believe you'd put up with that, Dad!" I cried. "If you had another woman coming *here* at Christmas . . .!"

"Al, cool it!" Lester said sternly.

Dad just sighed. "I've got to handle this in my own way, honey," he said. And walked slowly back to his room. He looked like an old, old man.

After I heard his door close and Lester closed his, I angrily wiped one arm across my eyes. *I* didn't have to trust Sylvia! *I* didn't have to excuse her! I rushed over to my chest, grabbed the picture of Miss Summers off my mirror – the photo of her I'd always liked best, Sylvia in a filmy blue and green dress – and ripped the picture in half.

"There!" I cried, and ripped it a second time. "There! And there! And there!" And then I lay face-down on my bed and bawled some more.

As Christmas drew near, our house was like a morgue, and I began to feel that as much as I had loved Sylvia Summers in the past, I hated her now. I was glad we were busy at the shop. I went in twice after school the week before the holiday, just to help out. I'd bought Polartec gloves for both Dad and Lester, as well as their favourite sweets. And I was going to make a chocolate cake for Christmas dinner, the best ever. But I knew that cake and gloves couldn't make Dad happy. I didn't have the power to do that for him, any more than he could make me forget Patrick. My anger at Sylvia was like a fever that wouldn't let up.

Elizabeth, however, seemed more relaxed these days somehow. I couldn't say she seemed happier, just thoughtful. Pamela and I didn't ask her any more about the episode with the biologist. To keep bringing the subject up would put more emphasis on it than it deserved. But when I saw her folks going in and out of their house, it bothered me that I knew something so basic about Elizabeth that they didn't.

On the last day of school, Sam Mayer wished me Merry Christmas, and I wished him Happy Hanukkah, and I was really surprised when Patrick called out, "Merry Christmas, Alice," as I was getting my coat out of my locker.

I took the chance to have a normal conversation. I smiled at him and said, "You, too, Patrick. Doing anything special?"

"I'm going skiing with my folks in Vermont."

"Sounds good," I said. "Happy New Year, too."

"Same to you," he said, and smiled that funny little smile that wrinkled the bridge of his nose. I told myself I still saw a glint in his eye for me, imagined or not, because I needed every glint I could get this Christmas.

Elizabeth and I walked home from the bus stop together. I'd told her what Karen had said about Jim Sorringer. I had to, because Karen had already told some of the kids on the bus. Karen is one of those people who seems to be your really close friend, but you never know.

"Well, if it will make your Christmas any happier, Alice, I told my folks," Elizabeth said.

"About Miss Summers? Why would that . . .?"

"No. About me. About what happened back in year three."

I stopped and looked at her. "Good for you, Liz!" I said. I gave her a hug right there on the pavement, and repeated, "Good for you!"

"And you were right. I feel *so* much better"

"What did they say?"

"Well, they were stunned. It wasn't that they didn't believe me. They never said that maybe I imagined it, but they quizzed me in such detail that I could tell they wanted to make sure. And then Mum cried. I *knew* she'd do that. They both kept saying, *Why didn't you* tell *us the first time?* That's the part they still can't understand. I can't, either. You just . . . when you're small, I think . . . you accept things about grown-ups, like whatever they do must be right because they're adults. There's so much they ask us to do anyway that we don't understand, so when this man told me I could help him not feel so lonely and asked me to stand still, well . . . it must be right, I figured, or my parents wouldn't have let me go on those walks."

"Kids can't reason like adults," I told her.

Elizabeth nodded. "What I feel worst about, though, is that . . . well, when I told my parents I thought they knew what their friend was doing to me, that's when Mum really cried. Dad even cried. But you know what? They hugged me. They both hugged me, just like you and Pamela did."

"You're lucky, Elizabeth, because you hear about girls telling their mums that their dads or stepdads are molesting them, and the mothers won't believe it. Don't want to believe."

"They made me promise that if anything like that ever happened again, I'd tell them. And best of all, they said I didn't have to tell the priest in confession unless I wanted. They said it was their friend who should have had to confess, not me. And it's like . . . like I'm twenty pounds lighter. I feel one hundred percent better."

"It must be a great feeling," I said, wishing I could feel the same about Sylvia Summers.

"The best! I don't even want to say the guy's name again. I'm going to call him *El Creepo*. Dad said that was fine with him."

We laughed a little.

"I did ask my parents, though, how a man who was supposedly loved by everyone and did such noble things could do something like that to a little girl, and they said that, unfortunately, a person can be mature in one way and infantile in another. He can be generous and selfish, both at the same time. And just because everyone seemed to love him didn't excuse what he did at all."

"I hope they also pointed out that a man who molests kids, no matter how wonderful he is, is breaking the law and, if he was still alive, would go to prison," I told her.

We got to Elizabeth's house and stopped. "The thing is," she said, "Mum's going to make an appointment with me to see a therapist. She wants to be sure I work out my feelings about El Creepo so that things won't bother me later on. I don't know how I feel about that."

"*I* think it's a great idea," I said. "I think it would make sense if we all had a head check once in a while. "

We were halfway through dinner that night when the phone rang. Dad had just put a bite of pork chop in his mouth, and gestured for me to get it, so I scooted my chair out from the table and went down the hall.

It was Sylvia's voice on the line, and she sounded tense: "Alice, I need to talk to Ben," she said right off "Is he there?"

"Yes," I said coldly. "I'll get him."

I clunked the telephone down on the hall table and hoped it hurt her ear. "It's Sylvia," I said in the kitchen. "She wants to talk to you."

Dad paused, his glass halfway to his lips. Then he hurriedly left the table, but I seethed.

Tell her this is the first year you've missed the Messiah Sing-along, I wanted to say to Dad. *All because it would have reminded you of her. Tell her how she's ruined Christmas for us, the whole Christmas season. Tell her she's a cheat, and that I take back all the good things I ever said to her.* I speared a potato and angrily thrust it in my mouth.

"Chew, Al," Lester said, even though I knew he was listening, too.

We both sat silently, trying to decipher what words we could hear of Dad's conversation.

"Sylvia? How are you?" Dad was asking.

There was a long silence. I heard the chair by the phone creak as he finally sat down. He still didn't say anything, and I could feel in my bones that this was goodbye. That she was going back to Jim Sorringer, and hadn't known how to tell him before.

"Swallow, Al," Lester said.

I swallowed the potato.

And then we heard Dad say, "Honey, I wouldn't have cared if you'd had dinner with him, but I think you handled it well." Lester and I looked at each other. "Of course! I can't help feeling sorry for the man." There was a long, long silence. Then, "I know . . . I feel the same way . . . You know I do . . . Yes, beyond a doubt." And finally, so soft and gentle, we could hardly hear it, "I can't wait until you're in my arms again."

Lester and I looked across the table at each other and suddenly we began to grin and gave each other a high five, just as Dad came back in the kitchen.

"Al," he said, "Sylvia wants to talk to you." He was smiling. His cheeks were pink, his eyes sparkled.

"Me?" I slowly lowered my hand, and could feel my face redden. I had talked to her with ice in my voice and slammed the phone down on the table. I'd torn her picture in pieces, for heaven's sake!

"What . . . what'll I say?" I choked.

"How about *Merry Christmas?*" Dad said, smiling still.

I went down the hall and picked up the phone.

"Alice, I want you to know what's going on," she said. "There was a Christmas concert at our school this afternoon, and when I got back to my flat, Jim Sorringer was waiting for me in the landlady's sitting room." And then, as though she was talking with a friend – she *was* talking with a friend – she said, "That is *so* like him. Just up and decides he's going to do something, and . . . I had no idea he was coming. He evidently thought he could change my mind about things by surprising me here, but I explained to him that I am madly in love with your dad, and I think he finally got the message. He's on his way back to London, to spend Christmas there. I know how stones get around, though, and wanted you to know that I had nothing to do with his visit. Nothing has changed between me and your dad."

"Oh, Sylvia! I love you! I really, truly do!" I cried. "Merry Christmas!"

"Well, sweetheart, I love you, too," she said, and I could hear the smile in her voice. "And I hope you have the best Christmas ever!"

When she hung up, I walked slowly to the kitchen and gazed unblinking at my family.

"Helloooo!" Lester said, waving one hand in front of me.

I blinked. "Dad," I said. "You know that picture I like of Sylvia? The one you took of her in her blue-green dress?"

"Yes, I know the one," Dad said.

"Could you get me another print? Something happened to the one I had."

Dad studied me for a minute. Then he said, "I suppose that could be arranged. What size did you want, Al? Four by six? Five by seven?"

"Poster size?" I said, and gave him a sheepish grin.

Here's an exclusive extract from the next Alice book —

Simply Alice

1

The Second Half

The thing about the second term of year ten is you're not so scared anymore. You know how everything works – your locker, the cafeteria queue, the buses, grades – and you don't go to school every day with your heart in your mouth, expecting to be humiliated half out of your mind.

Which, of course, makes it all the worse when it happens. Wearing an ankle-length beige skirt with a long-sleeved cotton T-shirt, I was coming out of the cafeteria with my two best friends, Elizabeth Price and Pamela Jones, heading for PE. on the ground floor. I'd had a hugely busy morning, starting with a meeting of the newspaper staff before school, and I still hadn't had a chance to duck into a toilet. After the big glass of orange juice I'd drunk for breakfast, and now the can of Sprite for lunch, I was in agony.

"Hey, guys, I've really, *really* got to go," I said as we

started towards the stairs. I could only walk in tiny, mincing steps.

"We'll be in the changing room in three minutes," Elizabeth said.

"I can't wait three minutes," I told her, looking around as we approached the stairs. "I thought there was a toilet on this floor, maybe just beyond . . ."

What happened next was like a home video on fast-forward. We must have been closer to the top step than I thought, because I was still looking around when suddenly I felt my body plunging forward, my books flying out in front of me.

I heard Elizabeth scream, "Oh, Alice!" and someone else shout, "Grab her!" and I could see the guys on the lower level look our way, but I was tumbling down the stairs, trying to grasp the railing as I went, and came to a stop on the second from the last step.

"Oh, my god!" Pamela yelled. "Are you hurt?"

I was pretty shaken, but within a few seconds I knew I wasn't hurt, not seriously – just bumps and bruises. My pride, mostly. I'd cut one knee, and my cheekbone stung. What I *was* conscious of was that my underwear and thighs were soaked, and it just kept coming. It was like someone had pulled a plug and I couldn't stop.

A tall guy had one hand under my back and another under my legs, and was lifting me to a standing position. "You okay?" he kept asking.

I wanted desperately for the earth to swallow me up, never to be seen again.

He must have felt the dampness because I saw him look behind me, like maybe I was broken and bleeding, and then he said gently, "My, my, my! That *did* scare the . . . uh . . . daylights out of you, didn't it?" He winked and walked away with the other guys, who didn't know what he was smiling about, and by that time Pamela and Elizabeth had reached the bottom of the stairs.

"Hide me," I choked.

"What? Are you all right? Are you hurt?" Elizabeth asked.

And then Pamela turned me around. "My god, Alice! You . . ." Trust Pamela to burst out laughing.

I backed up against the wall while kids stopped to pick up the pages of my ring-binder that were scattered all over the stairs. Then Pamela, walking ahead of me, and Elizabeth, walking behind, got me to the gym, and while the other girls played volleyball, I rinsed out my underwear and the back of my skirt, and held them under the blower to dry.

"Can anything be more humiliating than that?" I asked Elizabeth when we were showering later.

"You could have thrown up, too, while you were at it," she said.

At dinner that night, Dad said, "Al, what on earth happened to you?"

The left side of my face was bruised and swollen where I'd bumped against the stair rail. My real name is Alice Kathleen McKinley, but Dad and Lester, my twenty-two-year-old brother, call me Al.

"The most embarrassing thing that could possibly happen to a human being, that's all," I said, and launched into the whole dramatic story of how this handsome older boy had knelt down to help me up and had felt my wet skirt. "Nothing in the world could be more awful than that," I repeated.

"Wrong," said Lester, passing the lentils and sausage, which, for anyone who cares to know, looks like mud. "He could have gathered you up in his arms, clutched your body to his, gazed into your eyes, and *then* you wet your pants."

"Well, believe it or not, there are some things in life worse than humiliation," said Dad. He, of course, means death and dying and wars and starvation, but it's sort of hard to think about those things when you're tumbling down a flight of stairs and losing control of your bladder at the same time.

I guess it's natural that my dad sees the serious side of life, because my mum died when I was at nursery school, and I suppose you never get over something like that. But now he's engaged to my year eight English teacher, Miss Summers, and he's the happiest I've ever known him to be, even though she's on a teacher-exchange programme in England.

"So other than using the school stairs as a toilet, how was your day?" Lester asked me.

"Well, a nice thing *did* happen," I said. "Since I'm one of the year ten roving reporters for *The Edge*, and I'm also part of the stage crew for our spring musical, I'm supposed to write three articles on 'behind the scenes of a school production.' That should be fun."

"That's a great assignment," said Dad. "What musical?"

"*Fiddler on the Roof*."

"Oh, I like that one. Wonderful music!" Dad said.

"So what do *you* do, Al? Pull the curtain?" asked Les.

"All sorts of stuff," I told him. "Scene changes, props, costumes – wherever I'm needed."

"I'm glad to see you expand yourself a little. This may turn out to be a good year for you after all," said Dad.

What he means, of course, is that I may not go to pieces or jump off a bridge or anything, just because Patrick and I broke up this last autumn. Not that I would ever let somebody else make me so miserable that I'd do that. But it sure hadn't been an easy autumn, watching Patrick and Penny, the "new girl in town," kissing around school and doing all the things together that Patrick and I used to do.

But I'm trying to pay more attention to other people and not be so self-centred. So I turned to Lester and said, "How was *your* day?"

"Interesting," he said. "I had coffee with one of my philosophy tutors."

"The babe?" I said, knowing that one of his teachers was really attractive, or so he'd told me. "I thought staff weren't supposed to date students."

"Did I say 'date'? I said 'coffee,' Al. We talked . . . Besides, she's not actually a professor, just an assistant tutor. She'd *like to* be a regular member of the staff though, and she's got the brains to do it."

"You flirted, I'll bet," I said.

"That's not a crime. It's not even a minor offence"

"So . . . how old is she?" I wanted to know.

"A year or two older than I am, I suppose."

"Watch it, Les," I said, and grinned.

Dad was smiling, too. "Well, I had a letter from Sylvia today, and we're looking at July twenty-eighth to get married."

That was about the best news I'd had in two years. Two years of trying to connect the beautiful Sylvia Summers with my dad, and now they were really, truly, officially engaged, except that she didn't have a diamond or anything. Didn't even want one, Dad said.

"That's fabulous, Dad!" I said excitedly "I hope she has ten bridesmaids and a symphony orchestra."

He laughed. "A simple little ceremony, Al, for family and friends. That's just the way we want it."

I guess, since it's their wedding, they can have whatever they want, but after working so hard to get them to fall in love, *I* thought we deserved an orchestra. A chamber quartet, anyway.

I was about as busy as I could imagine myself being, now that they were starting auditions for *Fiddler on the Roof*. The stage crew met three times a week after school, and it would become every day when we got closer to production. Actually the stage crew was divided up into lots of little crews, but most of us were on more than one – lighting, sound, sets, costumes, make-up, props, publicity . . .

The real surprise was when Pamela told me she was dropping out of the drama club. I couldn't believe it. She's always talked about wanting to be an actress or a model, and she'd had the lead our play in year seven

"*Why*?" I asked, when she told me.

"I didn't know it was going to be a musical, and I don't think my voice is good enough for a leading role," she said.

"But you could be in the chorus, Pam! Or you could work behind the scenes. There's always something you could do."

"I don't want the chorus and I don't want to work behind the scenes. If I try out and don't make it, Mr Ellis will remember that when I audition next year or the year after that. When I try out for the first time, I want to knock his socks off, and I can tell I'm not that good yet. I don't want a second-rate part. I want a major role."

I couldn't understand the feeling, never having wanted to be the centre of attention that much.

"So I'm going to take voice lessons," Pamela finished. "Dad's already found a teacher for me and signed me up. But, listen! Elizabeth's got this great idea!"

We were on the bus going home, all squeezed together on one seat. Liz was by the window, I was in the middle, and Pam was on the end.

Pamela and Elizabeth were smiling. "Why don't the three of us sign up together as junior consultants for Tiddly Winks this spring!"

"Tiddly Winks?" I said in surprise. Tiddly Winks was an inexpensive earring shop that had recently expanded to include accessories of all kinds – hair stuff, hats, scarves, belts, shawls, necklaces . . . I tried to imagine myself a junior consultant. "What do you *do*?"

"It sounds really fun," Elizabeth assured me. "They're having a big promotion to advertise the new stuff in the shop, and they want people to come in for a colour and bone-structure analysis."

"*We're* supposed to do that?" I said. "What do I know about bone structure?"

"No, the professionals do that. Then they tell us what category the customer is in – like, she's a 'spring' or an 'autumn,' and 'angular' or 'round,' and then we show them all the colours and styles in her category."

"The thing is," Pamela continued, "we get points for every friend we bring in and points for every dollar each of our customers spends. When we get a certain number of points, we get free earrings or something."

"We're going to do it two evenings a week and on Sunday afternoons through the end of March," said Elizabeth. "We can all ride to the mall together."

I was beginning to feel squeezed in, and not just because I was sitting in the middle. "Hey, guys, I *can't!*" I said. "Between the Melody Inn on Saturdays and the newspaper and the stage crew, I'm stretched about as far as I can get already!"

"So give up the stage crew," said Pamela.

"*What*?"

"We joined the drama club together," she reminded me, "and now that I'm not going to try out, why don't you do Tiddly Winks with us? It's not as though you've got one of the major parts or anything. C'mon! Just tell them you don't want to do it, and sign up with Liz and me. We're going down tomorrow."

"I *can't!*" I croaked. "I already said I'd do it. I've been assigned to sets, props, and publicity."

"But that was when we thought we'd be going to rehearsals together," Pamela said. "Just tell them you changed your mind."

"But I *want* to do it!" I protested. "Just because you changed your mind doesn't mean *I* have to!"

Pamela seemed offended that I'd want to do something without her. "It's not as though you're the only one in school who can do the job, Alice. What's so important about being on the prop committee?" she asked.

"We could have so much fun together at Tiddly Winks!" Elizabeth said. "We'd have a blast. Of course, if you don't *want* to be with us . . ."

It did sound like it could be fun, but to tell the truth, the stage crew sounded better. I wasn't all that nuts about accessories. "I just can't," I said. "Don't be mad."

"Who's mad?" said Elizabeth, getting that look on her face. "I just thought it was *something* the three of us could do together – you're always so busy on the newspaper."

"*You* guys can still do it!" I said. "I'll come down and you can do a colour analysis on me."

"Whatever," said Pamela.

They'll get over it, I told myself. After all, Elizabeth hadn't joined the drama club when Pamela and I signed up, and we hadn't made a fuss about it.

For the first time, I was doing things on my own, and had made friends with another girl on the stage crew, in the year above, named Molly. She's shorter than I am, sort of squat, and wears overalls most of the time. Her hair is cut in a punk rock style, and she has the biggest, bluest eyes I've ever seen.

"So which of these things can you find?" Molly asked me the next day, after Mr Ellis had distributed a list of all the different props we'd need.

"Not many," I said.

"Me either," said Molly. "It would help if one of us were Jewish, because all the characters in the musical are. Where are we going to find all this stuff?"

"We start asking, begging, pleading, borrowing, and hope we don't have to sell our bodies or resort to stealing," I joked.

There was one other girl who joined the stage crew, from year twelve. Her name was Faith, and she was tall, rail-thin, wore long, gauzy dresses of purple or black with beaded waistcoats, black stockings, granny tie-up shoes with pointed toes, and lots of bracelets. Her hair was long and very straight, and she wore pale, almost white, face powder with her lips and eyes outlined in black.

We liked Faith a lot, but we didn't especially care for her boyfriend, Ron Blake. He'd hang around at the back of the room when we had meetings, and never let Faith out of his sight. She even told him when she was going to the toilet. When it was just the two of them in the cafeteria or out on the school steps, they cuddled a lot, and Ron gave her tender kisses. But when she was around other people – I don't know; Ron seemed jealous or something.

He was there again on Thursday when we met after school, slouched in a chair off to one side, while Faith and Molly and I were checking things off our lists.

Pretty soon I heard Ron say, "Hey! C'mere!"

I don't think Faith heard him, because we were busy deciding who was going to try to get waistcoats for the guys in the cast if they didn't come up with any themselves.

"Hey!" Ron said again, more loudly.

Faith glanced around and held up one hand, as if to signal, *Wait a minute*, and went on talking to us.

Ron got up from his chair and strode over to her. Faith looked up. "*What?*" she asked.

"Let's head out," he said, as though Molly and I weren't even there.

"I've got to finish here first," Faith answered.

He looked at his watch. "We leave here at four," he told her, and left the room.

Four wasn't time enough to do all we had to do, because we had each made a list of the props and clothes we were sure we could get, and those we still had to find. But this time when Ron came back he didn't call her name. He just walked up behind her, took hold of her long hair, and slowly tipped back her head until she was looking straight up at him.

"Owww!" she said, making a joke of it.

"Let's go," he said.

"Just a minute, Ron," she said, trying to work her hair free.

"*Now!*" he said.

Faith stood up, and he let go of her hair. "If you find any more of this stuff, call me, okay?" she said to us.

We nodded and Faith left, with Ron steering her by one shoulder.

Molly and I looked at each other. "I think maybe Faith has problems," I said.

"And he's number one," said Molly.